BELIZAIRE
THE CAJUN

BELIZAIRE
T H E C A J U N
A NOVEL

By Glen Pitre   Edited by Dean Shapiro

Pelican Publishing Company
Gretna 1988

For my parents, Emelia and Loulan

Copyright © 1988
By Glen Pitre and Dean M. Shapiro
All rights reserved

First printing, October 1988

Library of Congress Cataloging-in-Publication Data
Pitre, Glen, 1955-
    Belizaire the Cajun.

    I. Shapiro, Dean M., 1950-   II. Title.

PS3566.I845B4 1988   813'.54   88-9820
ISBN 0-88289-671-7

Manufactured in the United States of America
Published by Pelican Publishing Company, Inc.
1101 Monroe Street, Gretna, Louisiana 70053

Contents

Belizaire shows off the horse he got for Dolsin's present. (Photo by Michael Caffery)

Preface

IN THE MID-1700s, a tragic exodus with far-reaching consequences began.

Great Britain had taken over Canada's Atlantic provinces in the 1713 Treaty of Utrecht and had attempted, for the next forty years, to force its culture on the French-speaking Catholics of the Acadia region (Nova Scotia). The Acadians were pressured to give up their language, their religion, and their customs and swear allegiance to the British crown. Some of the Acadians did so and became Anglicized, but the majority of them refused.

Finally, in 1755, as Britain stood on the brink of yet another of its many wars with France, British authorities began rounding up the Acadians who refused to pledge loyalty to the crown. Thousands of Acadians were deported, often with nothing more than the clothes on their backs. In many cases, whole families were separated from one another. Thus were the Acadians forcibly exiled from a region they had colonized a century and a half earlier.

This period was the setting for Henry Wadsworth Longfellow's epic poem, *Evangeline*. Separated from her fiance during the Acadian exile, the heroine, according to legend, waited in vain for him to join her underneath an oak tree near what is today St. Martinville in southern Louisiana. While there may be some credibility to the legend, the real truth was much harsher for the exiles.

The British herded the Acadians onto ships, some just barely seaworthy, and scattered many of them in various locales along the east coast of North America. A large number of them found their way back to France where, for about thirty years, they lived on the fringes of French society as refugees, relegated to poverty, starvation, and neglect. Finally, when they had the opportunity to settle in a homeland of their own, they eagerly took advantage of it.

That homeland was the French-founded colony of Louisiana. At the time it had just come under Spanish rule, but Spain and France were allies against England, and the Spanish authorities permitted the Acadians to settle along the lower Mississippi River. There, just upriver from the small settlement of New Orleans, they found the haven they had long sought. They built their homes, followed their customs and religion, and spoke their own language, free from the harassment of others.

Some of the Acadian exiles from Nova Scotia had gone to Louisiana earlier and were already settled in. The majority followed in the 1780s. For years afterward, they lived their lives in peaceful isolation. They hunted in the abundant woods, fished the clear waters of the river and adjacent waterways, and grew crops in the fertile alluvial soil created by the river, confident that the homeland they had carved out for themselves would remain forever inviolate.

That blissful existence along the river, however, came to an end over a ten- to thirty-year period. As the plentiful sugarcane that grew in the region became a profitable cash crop, large plantations swallowed up the smaller homesteads. The Acadians—or ''Cajuns,'' as they had come to be known—began moving further westward.

This time their migration took them to the swamps and prairies that covered vast tracts of south Louisiana. They built their homes and villages in remote areas, many of which were only accessible by boat along narrow inland waterways called bayous. There they supported their families by hunting, fishing, and working small farms. Isolated from the rest of the world by forboding natural barriers, the Cajun culture developed and thrived, passing down a legacy that continues to this day.

Those who settled on the prairies where the soil was not conducive to farming took up raising cattle. This was something they had learned from the Spanish colonists of Mexico, a few of whom had settled in the region earlier. Soon after Louisiana achieved statehood in 1812, English-speaking settlers, moving westward, also discovered the prairies of the Attakapas (Acadiana) region of southwestern Louisiana. They came as planters at first, but they soon learned about ranching from the Cajuns. They brought in herds, fenced off huge sections of what had been open prairie, and forced many of the Cajuns out of their smaller homesteads.

As they continued adding to their own holdings, the English-speaking settlers became more and more hostile to the Cajuns, and vice versa. The differences in language, religion, and culture created a rift between the ''Anglos'' and many of the Cajuns who resented their presence.

Forced into the status of second-class citizenship by the encroachments of these wealthy ranchers, the descendents of the earlier Acadian settlers saw their prime hunting and grazing lands cut off from them. Many of them were reduced to stealing cattle from these land barons in order to survive and feed their poor families. There is ample evidence to suggest that such thievery was widespread across the prairies, and it added further to the bad blood that existed between the Anglos and the Cajuns.

In one recorded instance, a cattleman caught a rustler in the act of butchering a stolen cow and, when confronted by the irate rancher, the thief politely reminded the rancher that he had ''sold'' it to him. When the rancher angrily denied ever having sold the cow, the rustler told him that he could produce ''witnesses'' to the sale. These ''witnesses'' were friends and relatives of the rustler. Outraged, the rancher threatened to take the rustler to court, and the rustler invited him to do so.

The cattleman sought recourse through the judicial system, swearing out a warrant for the rustler's arrest. But, when the case came to court, true to his word, the rustler produced witnesses who swore under oath that they saw the rancher sell the cow to him. The jury, consisting of friends and relatives of the accused, voted to acquit him.

This was not an isolated incident. Other incidents similar to this were recorded throughout the Attakapas region. The cattlemen were in an uproar, seeing justice thwarted time and time again by a judicial system they had placed their faith in. Sheriffs, whose jobs it was to uphold the laws in their parishes, were usually helpless to do more than arrest the offenders, then watch them go free as "not guilty" verdicts were handed down by packed juries. In some instances the sheriffs themselves were believed to have been linked to the thieves—either by family ties or friendship.

In early 1859, cattlemen all across southwestern Louisiana decided to strike back. The result was a dangerous showdown that went well beyond the bounds of the law.

After more than thirty years of frustration at seeing their cattle stolen, their homes and barns burned and looted, and offenders going unpunished by the judicial system, many of the landowning citizens in several Louisiana parishes and municipalities banded together to form "Committees of Vigilance," sometimes known as "Regulators." Heavily armed, large in number, and fearsome in appearance, these vigilantes rode by night, issuing their ominous warnings and enforcing them with great severity if they went unheeded.

Led by military officers who were later to distinguish themselves in battle during the War Between the States, the Committees of Vigilance, for a brief time, reigned supreme in the parishes and municipalities of the Attakapas region. Many of their members were Cajuns themselves, and their targets were not only Cajuns. Blacks, both slave and free, who were considered to be troublemakers—along with their white sympathizers—were also singled out for punishment.

The vigilantes operated freely and openly and the identities of their members were known to the authorities. They administered the "justice" they claimed the courts had denied them, and their version of that "justice" was swift and unmerciful. It consisted first of an exile order for the offender, a flogging if he disregarded it, and the threat of execution if he failed to heed the first two warnings.

To the Cajuns in 1859, forced exile was an all-too-painful reminder of their roots. Many of them, whose families had forged an existence on their lands for generations dating back to the earliest Acadian settlements in the 1700s, lived in terror of the judgement of these night riders who operated at the behest of the cattle barons. Hundreds of families were tearfully forced to leave their ancestral homes and seek refuge in Texas. Others risked their lives in outright defiance. Some historians have even attributed executions to these vigilante organizations, though the evidence remains inconclusive.

A large group of opponents of the vigilantes, known as "Anti-Regulators," came into being following a proclamation by Governor Robert C. Wickliffe outlawing the Attakapas vigilance committees. On May 28, 1859, he ordered the committees to disband but they disregarded his warning, setting the stage for a showdown between the two factions.

That showdown came on September 3, 1859 as the anti-vigilantes gathered at a farmhouse along Bayou Queue de Tortue near Vermilionville (the present-day Lafayette). From there, a force of about 1,800 heavily-armed men planned to attack the town. However, word of the plan leaked out. A force of 700 vigilantes, wielding a four-pound brass cannon, surrounded the farm and thwarted the plan. The presence of heavy artillery on the side of the vigilantes was enough to frighten their opponents, most of whom fled. Many anti-vigilantes were captured, whipped, and and sentenced to leave the state after forcibly signing "confessions" acknowledging their "guilt." Thus, without a shot being fired that day, the Committees of Vigilance accomplished their objective. Their adversaries' power was broken and, having no purpose left to serve, the committees quietly disbanded.

Into this volatile and trigger-happy state of affairs came Belizaire Breaux, a Cajun medicine man—an herbalist and healer, a gentle, deeply-religious man of peace and compromise. It was to him that the Cajuns, many of whom had been ordered exiled by the Vermilion Parish Committee of Vigilance, turned to for comfort and guidance. He became their spokesman, their advocate and their unofficial leader. Ultimately, it was Belizaire who had to struggle to maintain the delicate balance between his love for his fellow Cajuns and the woman he loved who was married to one of the hated committee members.

The events described in this book are fictitious, bearing only peripheral resemblance to actual events. Any resemblance between characters in this work and actual persons living at that time is purely coincidental. Single characters are often a composite of several individuals.

In essence, this is the story of one man's struggle to keep himself above the fray while going about his and God's work of healing in the community, giving life rather than taking it, and maintaining his fierce loyalty to his people, whether they were right or wrong. This novelization follows as closely as possible the final shooting script for the feature film, ''Belizaire the Cajun'', written, directed, and co-produced by Glen Pitre for Cote Blanche Feature Films, Ltd. The movie was released for commercial showing in theaters around the world in 1986.

This book is not an attempt to single out particular individuals or groups for praise or condemnation. It does not moralize about who (if anyone) was right or wrong in the confrontations between the vigilantes and the alleged lawbreakers they condemned. It does attempt to put the turbulent events of that time in their proper perspective and show how they affected the lives of those described in these pages. Discerning readers can formulate their own judgements.

This book and the film it is based on are efforts to show the dangers inherent in allowing our cherished democratic institutions to degenerate to the point at which people begin taking the law into their own hands. It is a situation that has occurred many times throughout our history in many other regions and cities, and it still occurs even today.

Much of this material was gleaned from folktales passed on

from one generation to another, as well as from chronicles that survived and have been translated and reprinted since then. Readers interested in learning more about this turbulent era are directed to a book entitled *The Vigilante Committees of the Attakapas* by Alexandre Barde, written in French in 1861 and reprinted, in English, by Acadiana Press of Lafayette, Louisiana in 1981.

Other selections can be found in *The Attakapas Country: A History of Lafayette Parish* by Harris Lewis Griffin (Gretna, LA: Pelican Publishing Company, Inc., 1974).

DEAN M. SHAPIRO
EDITOR

Director and writer Glen Pitre (right) goes over the details of a funeral scene with members of the cast during filming of the movie Belizaire the Cajun. (Photo by Michael Caffery)

The Making of the Movie

THE IDEA FOR the movie began at a party in 1981. What started out as ''Belizaire's Waltz,'' later became ''Acadian Waltz,'' and finally ''Belizaire the Cajun.'' In the four years it took to get to the screen it went through a metamorphosis worthy of Cinderella.

I was on the Cajun movie tour in Lafayette, Louisiana when I ran into an old friend of mine, Richard Guidry, at a party. When the evening turned to storytelling, Richard told a tale handed down in his family. The story centered around a *traiteur* (treater), a Cajun faith and herbal leader, who had once been arrested and imprisoned for the murder of a vigilante. When he was later released, he moved in with the vigilante's widow.

I knew this was a good story and I began thinking more and more about it. I did some research on the vigilante movements of southwestern Louisiana in the 19th century and decided to move the story back to the year 1859 when vigilante activity had just started and was at its peak. I wrote the first few drafts of the screenplay ''on the road,'' while touring with my films in Canada and France. I wrote on trains, planes, and on friends' kitchen tables.

By the third draft, I began making plans for a slightly more ambitious Cajun movie. On another ''show and tell'' with my films in Houston, the organizer of the screening asked to see my script. He read it and liked it so much that he sent it in as his nominee to the Sundance Institute.

The Sundance Institute in Utah was founded by Robert Redford in 1979 to give a helping hand to promising young writers and directors working outside of the Hollywood studio system. For 1983, five feature projects were chosen from among 450 nominees—two from New York, two from California, and one from Cut Off, Louisiana—mine.

The first phase of the program was script development. I further reworked the script under the guidance of veteran screenwriters such as Bill Witliffe ("The Black Stallion" and "Country"), Tom Rickman ("Coal Miner's Daughter" and "River Rat"), and Waldo Salt ("Midnight Cowboy" and "Coming Home").

Next came the June Laboratory, held at Sundance. On my arrival, as I was standing around, gawking at the mountains (which we don't see too much of in south Louisiana), this blonde-haired fellow comes up to me and shakes my hand, saying, "I really like your films." When I realized it was Robert Redford, I nearly panicked. I thought to myself, "I'm supposed to telling *him* that."

At the June Lab, I actually got a trial run for the shooting of the picture. Sundance provided a cast and video crew for me to shoot half the scenes in the script. Accompanying me to the set were veteran directors such as Sidney Pollock ("Tootsie") and Karl Malden, the great actor. It would have been a dream for me to watch these people direct, yet here they were watching *me* direct, giving me pointers, and letting me peek inside their bag of tricks.

The labs also encompassed, in addition to more script work, one-on-one meetings with virtually every specialty involved in the production of the film. My co-producer, Allan Durand, and I met with editors, cameramen, production managers, film composers, distributors, and even attorneys. Each of them gave advice and pointers from their areas of expertise, all tailored to the production of "Belizaire."

Actress Gail Youngs, who had appared in such films as

"Rumors of War" and "The Stone Boy," was cast by Sundance for the role of Alida, the Cajun woman torn between Belizaire and the vigilante son of a rich plantation owner. Her work so impressed Allan and I that we cast her on the spot. The commitment she made to us then held for the two years it took to finally get the shooting underway.

Later on, Gail's husband, Oscar Award-winner Robert Duvall ("Tender Mercies" 1983), came on board as a creative consultant. This was, of course, a great honor for us. Duvall had appeared in such classics as "The Godfather," "Apocalypse Now," and "The Great Santini," and had directed the box office hit "Angelo, My Love." While on location for the shoot in Louisiana, he also played a cameo role as the preacher at Matthew Perry's funeral.

Not long afterward, we signed Armand Assante to take on the title role as Belizaire. The key elements were now in place and we were ready to begin the job of financing the picture. Allan and I decided we wanted to keep the movie "home-grown" and raise the money entirely in Louisiana. It was a decision that nearly ended in tragedy.

On my first trip to meet with potential investors, an oncoming car lost control and smashed into me head-on. It took 45 stitches to close up the cuts I sustained across my eyebrows, and my ribs were badly bruised as well. It took the people in my office three days to get up the nerve to tell me that ten minutes after I left, the investors had called to cancel the meeting.

When my wounds healed, I continued the task. With the help of Allan, Executive Producer Jim Levert, Associate Producers Paul Hardy (now Lousiana's Lieutenant Governor), George Graham, and Jacob Landry, we raised the money. The investors included doctors, lawyers, businessmen, sugarcane farmers, crawfish processors, an elementary school teacher, and even two competing manufacturers of hot pepper sauce. Very few of them had ever put money into a film before, and the entire fundraising process took fifteen months. The final $50,000 came in on a grant from the National Endowment for the Arts.

It was the home-grown Cajun aspect of "Belizaire" that built up the community support, the "labor-of-love" enthusiasm that allowed the project to get off the ground. We did not have a large budget to work with and thousands of man-hours went into the production, much of it by volunteers. Everything from horses and buggies to entire restored villages were donated for the film's use. One rancher whose cattle we used, even went so far as to cut the plastic ear tags off 200 of his steers so they would look authentic, and he didn't even ask for a fee.

The same spirit engulfed the out-of-towners. The principal members of the cast were willing to forego their usual Hollywood fees for union minimums. They came down early to meet the people, learn the accent, pick up a bit of the local French, and familiarize themselves with the bayou country the shoot would be taking place in.

With the locations secured, pre-production began. The crew was hired, sets were built, arrangements for props and livestock were made, and casting for the other roles got underway. A few of the roles were cast in New York, but a majority of the choice parts went to Louisianians. Some of the people, such as my father who played the sheriff, had been in my earlier films, and others were cast at open calls. One casting session in Lafayette drew 2,500 people.

That stage of making a picture is funny. You've been dragging it along behind you for years, then . . . whoosh . . . it's got a life of its own. There are all these people, some of whom you don't even know, working to make your dream come true.

"Belizaire the Cajun" was shot in thirty-six days, beginning April 22, 1985 and ending on June 1. We used over 300 extras, 200 head of cattle, and three dozen horses. More than 250 "Acadian" costumes were sewn by a crew of seamstresses, many of them volunteering their services and working round the clock. A professional herbalist was brought in to gather and prepare the herbs Belizaire used for his medicines. Props, many of them antiques, were gathered from people's attics. Other props, when they couldn't be found, were specially made. Even the spider webs

Belizaire used to heal the whip scars on Hypolite Leger's back had to be "manufactured" when the real things couldn't be found.

Five separate locations were used. The Acadian Village, a tourist attraction near Lafayette, was used as the setting for the town where much of the film took place. Maison Acadienne (the Acadian House), in Longfellow Evangeline State park near St. Martinville, was used as the site of the Perry plantation with the huge "Gabriel Oak" dominating the front lawn. This was said to be the site of where Evangeline, heroine of Henry Wadsworth Longfellow's epic poem of the same name, waited in vain for the arrival of her beloved Gabriel after the Acadians (Cajuns) were expelled from Canada in 1755.

The Harris Broussard ranch was used for the shots of the cattle during the roundup scene, and the three-mile-long road to the Oak and Pine Alley Plantation was used for the buggy ride where James Willoughby and Old Perry argued over Matthew Perry's fitness to run the plantation. Some of the movie's most dramatic scenes, however, were shot in the Cypress Island/Lake Martin Swamp. This was where the vigilantes chased Hypolite Leger and murdered him. It was also the most dangerous and difficult location we used. Areas had to be carefully checked before the actors could race their horses into these muddy waters of uncertain depths. When the actors went in there on foot, they were entirely on their own, taking their chances with water moccasins and other dangerous swamp creatures. More than once some of the actors went in over their heads and disappeared—momentarily. Two camera boats and a fleet of support boats did some of the filming of these scenes, but much of the crew still had to work afoot in chest waders with hand-held cameras.

In all, the making of "Belizaire" was a memorable experience. I had done other films before, but never anything as extensive and technically involved. Even after the film was finally shot, edited, and prepared in its final form, the work didn't end there. We then had to contend with the mechanics of distribution, licensing, publicity, and many other facets of getting the movie to the attention of critics and moviegoers. It was an official selection of the

Cannes Film Festival in 1986, and it ran in movie houses all over the U.S. and abroad for a year. From there it went onto cable and home video, and eventually it may be seen on independent and network TV stations.

It was a long road and a hard one, but one I'll never forget. Making a movie and taking it from the germination of an idea to a finished product is a uniquely satisfying experience. There will undoubtedly be others for me, but the first one will always be the one I remember the most. I am grateful for and deeply indebted to all those who helped make it possible.

GLEN PITRE

Acknowledgments

To THE CAST from, bless his heart, Armand Assante, down to the farmer or housewife who spent an afternoon in a costume in the heat for a souvenir T-shirt and a chance to be in a movie; to the crew, who laughed at fatigue (sometimes maniacally) and managed to get every penny of our budget up on the screen; to the investors, for believing and putting their money where their mouths were; to the people of Sundance, from Robert Redford and his vision, to the late Waldo Salt and his wisdom, to Dede Madsen and her smile; to Mike Doucet, Beausoleil, and Howard Shore, for producing our Grammy-nominated soundtrack; to Paul Hardy and Jim Levert, for helping sell the idea; to Tom Skouras and George Pilzer, for getting the picture into theatres, video stores, and TV sets nationwide, and from Japan to Finland to Australia; to Richard Guidry, who first told me a tale of a healer run afoul of vigilantes, and Dean Shapiro, who coaxed that story, many incarnations later, into the form you find here; to the National Endowment for the Arts, who kicked in some cash; to Tom Simms, who helped from afar; Daisy Guidry, who held down the fort; Randall LaBry, on board from the first; Tesa Forlander, who kept it all organized; Allan "Sprinky" Durand, whose charm, energy, and shameless pride in what we had wrought carried us from Cut Off to Cannes; Jill Fitzpatrick, for her incredible

21

patience in putting up with me through all of it; and finally, to my parents, for their own patience, support, and encouragement, but mostly for never having taught me that some things are impossible.

SOUTHWESTERN LOUISIANA
1859

Armand Assante is Belizaire the Cajun, a lover, a fighter, a man of music, and a man of healing. (Photo by Michael Caffery)

CHAPTER ONE

Negotiating a Penance

"TRY TO AVOID the near occasion of sin," the young priest behind the screen whispered. The dark-bearded man kneeling in the confessional had his head bowed in reverence. "And, for your penance, say the rosary five times. Now make a good act of contrition."

"Five rosaries?" the bearded man questioned in astonishment. "Father, I have never in my life had the occasion to have to say three rosaries; let alone five. One or two, but . . ."

"Belizaire," the priest scolded, "The penance comes from God. It is not something you negotiate. Now make a good act of contrition," he added as a final warning.

Belizaire neither argued nor acknowledged the warning as he raised his right arm and lightly touched his forehead, his abdomen, and both shoulders in the sign of the cross. The priest then granted him the absolution he had come to receive, but the severity of the penance remained an issue as he stepped out of the confessional. At the same time the priest left the adjoining chamber.

Belizaire, dressed in a white shirt and tie, strode down the center aisle of the church, a few steps ahead of the priest, a hat in one hand and his leather pouch slung over his shoulder. "Belizaire," the priest called out in a whisper.

The bearded man kept walking.

"Belizaire," the priest called again, this time in a whisper so loud it disturbed the meditations of two elderly women sitting quietly in a pew. They looked up to see Belizaire stop in his tracks and turn to face the priest midway down the aisle.

A pained expression came over the handsome young cleric's face as he rotated his shoulder, showing Belizaire where it hurt. Belizaire looked at him with an expression of mild contempt; the tables were turning in his favor. The priest lowered his arm and addressed Belizaire in a manner that wouldn't distract the few parishioners who had come to pray for blessings from God.

"Belizaire," the priest whispered, "The medicine you gave me for my shoulder really helped me a great deal. Do you have any more?"

A disdainful expression still on his face, Belizaire clutched at the strap of the bag that hung low from his shoulder. He studied the priest.

"Yes, I do. I do," Belizaire answered. "I have one bottle left and that's promised to Madame Marais." He paused to let his words sink in before continuing.

"Of course, I could make some more . . . But I am going to be on my knees all day saying those five rosaries," he added, turning to go.

Belizaire strode toward the front door. "Belizaire! Belizaire!" the priest cried, following him and turning him around again. Once again, the two old women looked up. "The penance comes from God," he pleaded apologetically. "I only exercise a slight discretion in determining what it is."

"Well, my power to heal comes from God directly, and I have a great deal of discretion," Belizaire said, starting to get angry and shaking his finger under the priest's nose. "If I only had one rosary to say, I might have the time to make the medicine you need for your shoulder."

The look on the priest's face was a mixture of fear, frustration, and plaintiveness, combined with the physical pain he was enduring. "Belizaire, think of the bishop. He doesn't understand how things are run in these country parishes. If he heard you and

I were negotiating a penance, do you realize what he'd do to me?''

"Maybe you should talk to the bishop about your shoulder," Belizaire retorted, shrugging his own shoulders indifferently for effect, and then continuing his long stride toward the front door.

The priest addressed him twice by name again, in another loud whisper. Belizaire turned to look at him, holding up an index finger: "one rosary." The priest responded by holding up three fingers in front of his vestments: "three rosaries." Belizaire shook his head and continued holding up the single index finger. He was going to win this one; he felt sure of it.

The priest looked apprehensively to his right at the two elderly women praying. Seeing that they were unaware of what was going on, he shook his head in resignation and held a single finger discreetly in front of him.

Belizaire walked back over to him, pressing a small bottle of elixir into his hand. Clutching the priest's hand, he uttered, "Bless you." Belizaire continued to stride triumphantly out of the small country church. Stepping outside into the bright sunlight, he squinted and shielded his eyes before going to a nearby hitching post and untying his white mule. Climbing aboard the slow-moving animal, he rode through the streets of Abbeville toward his cabin out where the woods met the prairie, well past the outskirts of town.

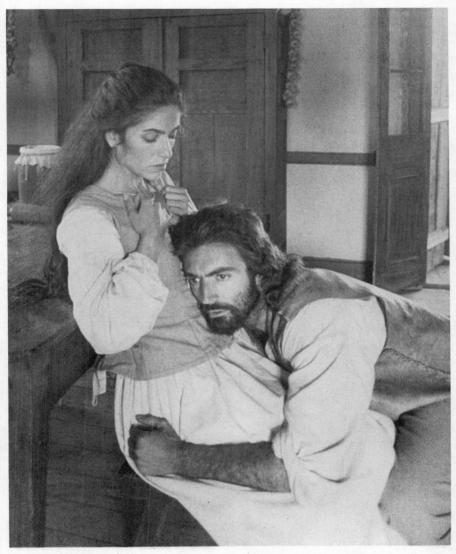

Belizaire listens to the sounds of Alida's (Gail Youngs) unborn child. (Photo by Michael Caffery)

CHAPTER TWO

"The Sickness that Foretells What's Coming"

THE NINE YEAR-OLD boy in the straw hat had been waiting impatiently for several hours. "Mr. Belizaire?" he called softly from the front porch of Belizaire's cabin, when he heard the healer's arrival.

Belizaire turned and looked up from the mule he was tethering in his front yard. He ducked under the rope holding the mule to a nearby tree and headed toward the young voice. It was Dolsin, Alida Thibodaux's oldest son.

"My momma is sick," the boy went on, as Belizaire stepped onto the porch and stood in front of him. "The sickness that foretells what's coming."

The young boy couldn't guess why his news brought a misty look to Belizaire's eyes. He didn't know, either, that the sickness he spoke of was morning sickness, that what was coming was a baby, or that Belizaire was letting himself daydream for a moment that it could have been his.

Belizaire continued to stand silently in front of Dolsin. "She said you'd know about it," the boy concluded, hanging his head low.

Without a word, Belizaire entered his unpainted cypress cot-

tage with the boy closely behind. The interior was magical, packed
with strange plants, herbs, and roots hanging from the beams of
the low ceiling. On a table in the kitchen were more herbs and
plants waiting to be processed. All around were patent medicine
bottles filled with liquids of varying colors, a mortar and pestle for
grinding, and other tools of the healer's craft.

Belizaire selected some dried red raspberry and fresh citronella
and packed them into his pouch. He slid several bottles of tisanes
and remedies into the pockets of a leather belt for the other deliv-
eries he would have to make afterward. He rolled and tied it all up
as the boy explored the room. Objects of mystery were every-
where. Belizaire's mysterious armoire held many objects of fascination whose functions Dolsin knew nothing about. At the same
time, the boy reverently looked over at the man, the renowned
healer he had come to bring back with him.

"Hey, Dolsin?" Belizaire called to the boy. Dolsin looked up as
Belizaire raised his arms and pushed aside some plants hanging
from the ceiling. Taking hold of a root tied to one of the rafters,
Belizaire twisted and broke off a piece of it, tossing it to the boy.

"Chew on that," Belizaire told him.

The boy caught and placed the root in his mouth, biting down
on it. The sweet taste of sassafras bark made his palate tingle.

Dolsin's fingers curiously explored the accordian on the man-
tle. He had never seen one before. It was a strange instrument,
new to the prairie. It was said that Belizaire had been given it by a
German farmer at Robert's Cove. The man had been nearly dead
of the "Strangers' Disease," when Belizaire revived him and
saved his life. The grateful farmer paid the healer with his prized
possession, his accordian.

Reaching down to pick up his bag, Belizaire swung it over his
shoulder, and marched out. Dolsin silently followed him.

Belizaire and Dolsin walked along a path straddling a thin neck
of land between two shallow ponds. Their presence scared up a
grosbec, and Belizaire smiled as he watched it fly off. He did not
need to hunt; his patients provided him with all the game he
needed. He could appreciate the bird for the beauty of its flight

without the reflex of reaching for the powder horn his neighbors might feel.

Belizaire and Dolsin reached the small path along the bayou that led to the small cabin Dolsin shared with his parents and younger brother and sister. The land was higher here, more suitable for farming than the prairies where a clay pan three feet down meant poor drainage.

Belizaire remembered when farmhouse after farmhouse lined this bayou. Now, however, most of those small "habitations" had been bought up and consolidated into plantations like the Perry place, belonging to Dolsin's grandfather. He was his grandfather even if he wouldn't admit it.

Arriving at the boy's house, Belizaire entered and cordially greeted his mother, Alida. She was clad in a yellow chiffon housedress that reached down well below her ankles, and her long brown hair was tied into a single braid that draped lazily over her left shoulder.

Though no longer the beautiful young *fille* who had broken the hearts of many young bayou men (including Belizaire's) when she fell in love with a non-Cajun, Matthew Perry, Alida retained some of that same allure. Three children had added a few lines to her face, but they took nothing away from her overall attractiveness—least of all to Belizaire himself.

Belizaire directed her to a chair and had her lean back against the kitchen table. Kneeling on the floor in front of her and gently laying his left ear on her fully-clothed belly, he listened attentively for whatever faint signs of life his trained senses could detect.

Even after he had heard all there was to hear, he continued to listen. Too much efficiency could lose him the confidence of his patient. Besides, even after a decade, the scent Alida gave off still intoxicated Belizaire. He lingered longer. When he thought he had listened long enough, he stood up.

"Well," he began, looking her full in the face, "You don't have the sunstroke and you don't have the moonstroke. You'll have another boy, Alida."

She looked up at him and let out a soft laugh.

"Sometime between Christmas and the New Year, I believe," Belizaire went on, walking around the table where she was seated and laying out some of his bottles and herbs. Belizaire selected a bunch of green plants and placed them aside as he began loading the other objects back into his sack. "Some of that red raspberry ought to make you fine," he said.

Smiling and shaking her head, Alida stood up. "Morning sickness near sundown," she said wistfully, tying an apron around her slim waist. "I was always a little . . ."

"Contrary?" Belizaire interrupted, finishing the sentence for her. Holding up the remedies he had selected and laying them down again on the table, he continued packing his bag. Alida began kneading the batch of corn dough she would bake into this week's bread for her family.

"Good. Thank you," Alida sighed as her knuckles dug into the thick dough she was working on, softening it up for baking. "Promise not to tell anybody," she added.

"What?" Belizaire asked, looking at her with a puzzled expression.

"I know I can't keep the secret forever, but . . ." Alida started to say.

"Matthew has to act right by you now, no matter what his poppa says," Belizaire interjected.

"It's good of you to care." Alida sighed again, bringing over another ball of dough and placing it on the table in front of her.

"I do care. I care much more than you know, Alida," Belizaire replied, the sadness in his voice betraying long-buried emotions.

She giggled like a young girl and shook her head at his flattery as she sprinkled a handful of yeast on the dough her hands were rolling and softening. He sat down and added a small helping of sugar to a cup of herbal tea in front of him. A wry smile escaped through his beard at her amusement.

"Belizaire," she said, shaking her head and smiling, "No wonder I hear such stories about you."

"What stories?" he asked, stirring the tea with the sugar spoon.

"What stories?" she replied playfully, mocking him. "You know . . . the widow Comeaux?"

"The widow Comeaux?" Belizaire repeated. "Why, she'd marry my mule if he'd have her."

"Belizaire," she giggled again, shaking her head at his response.

The whinnying of horses and sound of men approaching outside interrupted their conversation. "It's Matthew," Alida said, a trace of fear in her voice.

Outside, Matthew Perry rode up to his gate with two companions. The slouch hat looped around the back of his neck exposed his blond hair and boyish features. Matthew held a small pail of milk at his side which was still three-quarters full, despite the sloshing it took on the ride. Accompanying him was Amadee Meaux, the ranch foreman employed by Matthew's father, and his brother-in-law, James Willoughby, who stayed on his horse and waited outside the gate.

"Hey Meaux, get that for me will you?" Matthew said as he approached the gate. Meaux hopped down and opened it. Matthew rode his black pony into the enclosure.

"Better not take too long in there," Willoughby shouted after him.

A few drops of milk slopped out of the pail as Matthew cantered toward Dolsin, the first of his children to greet his arrival. "Hey, hey, how you doing podna?" he asked. Dolsin stood by quietly, waiting for his father to dismount.

"I'll give you the milk in a second. I got some stuff," Matthew continued.

Hopping off his horse, Matthew handed the pail to Dolsin. "Take that will you," he said as his seven-year-old son Valsin came walking up slowly. "How you doing buddy?" Matthew asked Valsin, who was handed the pail by his older brother. Dolsin eagerly mounted Matthew's horse and rode it to the feeding trough. His father continued toward the house, kneeling to greet four-year-old Aspasie, his daughter. He said a few words to the little girl and continued walking toward the house.

Standing nervously by the kitchen window, Alida turned and addressed Belizaire. "Promise me. Don't tell Matthew about the baby."

Belizaire placed his hand over his heart and nodded his head in agreement. He scratched his beard and stared at the cup of tea in front of him.

Matthew climbed the three short steps to his porch as Alida pushed aside the curtain to step out and greet him. As she hugged him, behind his back Matthew began shaking a bag of pecans he had brought for her. The sound stirred her curiosity.

"What is that, Matthew?" Alida asked, giggling as he toyed with her.

"Something special. Something special for you," he answered, stringing her along.

"Sounds like pecans," she said, trying to look behind his back. He began passing them around his body, playing a cat and mouse game with her. She spotted them.

"It is pecans!" she cried, reaching for them.

In the kitchen, Belizaire stood up and slung his bag over his shoulder. He stuck his head through the curtain as Matthew and Alida were embracing and teasing each other, but he quickly withdrew it, respecting their privacy. Matthew saw him and his mood changed abruptly from playful to serious.

"What is that, the horse doctor in here?" he said, stepping from Alida's embrace and flinging the curtain aside.

"Matthew, I wasn't feeling well this morning," Alida said as her husband entered the house to investigate.

"What are you doin' in here?" Matthew grilled Belizaire as he entered the room.

"Well, as one with power to heal, Matthew, I've always had the good fortune to be able to enter any home I please," Belizaire replied.

He walked over and touched Alida lightly on her abdomen. "Just a little malady, Matthew . . ." she started to explain.

"I sensed a little stress here in the stomach region so I suggested some red raspberry and that citronel tea," Belizaire continued, pointing toward the table. Matthew, unsatisfied with the explanation, started to protest. Belizaire ignored him and continued.

"It's amazing that some people nowadays have so little respect for our Acadian ways, yet when one falls ill, they always seem to come back to me," Belizaire said.

"Monsieur Belizaire brought me herbs to calm my stomach. I'm just fine," Alida said.

Matthew touched Belizaire lightly on the shoulder. "Thank you, Belizaire. We'll be just fine," he said. "Now, I'd appreciate it if you'd get out," he went on, ushering Belizaire through the doorway.

Belizaire stepped onto the porch and Matthew followed to enforce his order. Instead of going down the steps, Belizaire stopped and drew a cross with his fingers on one of the porch posts. Then he pounded the post twice with the flat part of his right hand and was about to do it a third time when Matthew caught him by the wrist.

"What the hell are you doing?" Matthew quizzed him impatiently.

"This is to knock the pain out of your house, Matthew," Belizaire replied.

"Thank you very much, but I don't need the pain knocked out of my house. I appreciate that, though," Matthew sneered.

"Well, it's also good for snakes," Belizaire answered, pointing to the ground where a large water moccasin slithered away from the house. The snake had come from under the porch and was making its way across the yard. When he saw it was safe, Belizaire descended the three steps and began to walk away.

"Get away from here!" Matthew shouted menacingly as Belizaire crossed the yard. "Don't you come around here again! You're not needed around here!"

Belizaire continued walking, not answering or looking back. He passed Dolsin standing quietly alongside the henhouse. Hands defiantly on his hips, Matthew continued his tirade.

"I don't want to see you back here again! Do you hear me, Mr. Belizaire Breaux?" he shouted. Alida inconspicuously slipped back through the curtain into the house, not wishing to arouse his wrath further.

As Belizaire reached the gate, Willoughby was blocking his way and looking down at him with snide contempt.

"You still casting *gris-gris* spells, Belizaire?" Willoughby asked sarcastically.

Belizaire glared up at him from across the fence. "*Gris-gris* are for evil, Mr. Willoughby," he answered. "A man like you might well have use for them. But my powers are to heal."

"We had a San Domingo slave woman who dealt in magic," Willoughby said, placing his foot on the top of the gate. "We sold her off," he added, as if issuing a warning.

Belizaire mockingly raised his right hand and pointed his fingers toward Willoughby. "*Gris-gris, patasa! Gris-gris, patasa!*" he chanted ominously, scaring Willoughby who quickly moved his horse away from the gate.

"Don't you put no curse on me, Belizaire," he cried out, protectively holding a little red Bible in front of his face as he backed his horse off. Belizaire calmly opened the gate and sauntered out of Matthew's yard.

Back in the house, Matthew and Alida kissed each other lightly on the lips. Their whispered endearments were interrupted. "Matthew, hurry up in there!" Willoughby's impatient shout was heard in the distance. Alida turned sadly toward the window with her hands lightly on Matthew's shoulders.

"Hey," Matthew said, looking down sadly. "I have to go out again tonight."

"Again?" she asked, lightly touching him on the chest, her voice touched with sorrow.

"It'll be different now," he replied softly, looking down and stroking her neck with his hand. Raising his head he looked into her face. "The meetings are over. Tonight we ride."

CHAPTER THREE

The Night Riders

THE OMINOUS SOUND of thundering hoofbeats ripped through the still air, silencing the night birds that called to each other from widely scattered trees. Torches blazing, guns at the ready, the group of a dozen well-dressed, unmasked vigilantes ranging in age from their twenties to their sixties, galloped between the live oak trees, intent on the mission that brought them out that night.

Their first stop was the Leger cabin, a rude shack with a palmetto roof and walls. "Hypolite Leger!" the vigilante captain shouted as they entered the yard of Belizaire's nineteen-year-old cousin. "Hypolite Leger!" the captain shouted again.

Inside his cabin, Leger was startled by the strange sounds of hoofbeats and the snorting of nervous, tired horses. "*Qui c'est-que ca*? Who's there?" he muttered after hearing his name a second time. The noise had woken him from a deep sleep. The light of a dozen torches in his yard flickered through his window. Staggering onto his porch clad only in a thin coverall made from a flour sack, fear showed through Leger's youthful, bearded face.

Illuminated by torchlight, the riders wheeled their mounts into a circle around their spokesman, reining them in nervously. Leger studied the uncovered faces. Matthew Perry, James Willoughby, Amadee Meaux, and nine other men had come to pronounce his "sentence."

Matthew Perry (Will Patton) reluctantly rides with the vigilantes. (Photo by Michael Caffery)

"What have you men come here for?" Leger shouted, his voice trembling.

The vigilante captain struggled to hold his horse in check with one hand while he unrolled a scroll with the other and read from it.

"Hypolite Leger, you will undergo an infamous punishment because you have taken part in all the crimes which have desolated the country for many years!" the spokesman announced. "No longer having faith in our juries, mauled as they are by sheriffs who keep away honest men and admit rascals to the jurors' bench, we have formed ourselves into juries! You have been found guilty of theft and barnburning! You have been condemned to leave this state within two weeks!"

"I ain't done nothin'. I don't want no trouble," Leger shouted back, his voice still heavy with fear, but showing the first seed of defiance.

"If you break this bond, you will be hanged!" the captain warned, disregarding Leger's plea. "Let's go!" the spokesman commanded, and the twelve men wheeled their horses around, galloping off in the direction of the next settler.

Frozen to the spot, his heart pounding furiously, Leger watched as the torches silhouetted the riders racing off between the trees, ducking low under overhanging branches. In minutes, the lights and the thundering hoofbeats faded into the night. For a moment, Leger wondered if it had been a dream. Then he saw in the moonlight bathing his yard that the dust raised by the vigilantes' horses had not yet settled.

****

Galloping into another yard, torches still blazing, the vigilantes again wheeled their horses into a circle around their captain. "Felix Nunez!" the captain shouted as they came to a halt before another crude wooden cabin.

A dark-bearded man, naked from the waist up and looking half-asleep, appeared in the doorway. He was shadowed by his wife in a long nightgown and sleeping cap, a long brown braid hanging loosely over her left shoulder.

"Felix Nunez!" the captain began, unrolling his scroll. "You have been condemned to leave the state within two weeks! Go elsewhere and seek a living by work and morality! If you break this bond you will be hanged!"

Nunez stared blankly at his adversaries, his wife clutching his arm apprehensively. "Tell them to leave," she whispered. "They're scaring the children."

"Let's go!" the captain shouted, waving his scroll in the air, and the night riders galloped off after him. Nunez and his wife silently watched them ride off.

****

Farther up the road, a frightened Leger raced into Belizaire's cabin, waking him with panicked cries. "Hurry up, Belizaire! Hurry up!" Leger shouted, running in and out in confusion.

"Slow down, Hypolite," Belizaire replied, evidently annoyed at being awakened. Pulling his shirt over his bare chest on the run, Belizaire followed Leger into the yard. The two of them raced out to the road, but they stopped short at the pounding of approaching hoofbeats. Belizaire reacted swiftly, pulling Leger down into a nearby ditch that was covered with thick vegetation.

"Get down! Get down! Get down!" Belizaire whispered sternly, throwing his arm over his cousin's shoulder and pulling him lower. The horses and their riders thundered closer, drowning out the sound of Belizaire's and Leger's heavy breathing, and the vigilantes rode by without seeing them.

"They comin' for you too, Belizaire!" Leger whispered fearfully.

But the vigilantes rode on, passing Belizaire's cabin. "They didn't come for you!" Leger said as the sound of the horses faded in the distance. It was almost an accusation.

"I guess they'll come back for me later," Belizaire replied apologetically.

"We've got to warn Parrain!" Leger cried frantically, spring-
ing out of the bushes and running in the same direction as the
vigilantes. Belizaire emerged close behind him.

Racing through the woods, the two of them arrived at the cabin
of Leger's godfather, whom he affectionately called "Parrain."
Running onto the porch and awakening Parrain and his family,
Leger frantically told the bare-chested, balding, middle-aged man
about the vigilantes' warning earlier that evening.

"They came to my house!" Leger began as Parrain leaned
against his front door, lightly touching Leger's chest, trying in
French to calm him down.

"They didn't say anything about the sheriff! They just said I
have to go! They said I did things I didn't do! I didn't do it!"
Leger went on as Parrain still tried to calm him.

Standing close by, Parrain's bare-chested sixteen-year-old son
listened and watched as Belizaire nervously paced the length of the
porch. Belizaire lifted his hand and signaled for quiet.

"Sssshhh," he whispered as the sound of hoofbeats drew closer.

The vigilantes, torches still blazing, dashed into the yard and
stopped. Parrain positioned himself in his doorway, propped
against the posts, ready to close the door and barricade it if neces-
sary. On the porch nearby, his son, Belizaire, and Leger stood
silently, awaiting the "verdict" the dozen armed men had come to
pronounce.

"Telephor Plaisance! Telephor Plaisance!" the vigilante captain shouted from a short distance away. "You will undergo an
infamous punishment because you've taken . . ."

Before he could finish reading from his scroll, Parrain's teenage
son Jean rushed toward the group, waving his bare arms in the air
and screaming, "Get out! Just get out!"

Jean charged one of the mounted men and pushed his horse
back a few steps. The vigilante swung out with his foot and kicked
the boy, who sprawled onto the ground, hands over his head and
grimacing in pain. Guns clicked as a dozen nervous men prepared
themselves for an armed confrontation.

"Hey, get back!" Belizaire shouted as he ran forward, pulling Jean gently to his feet.

"That's Belizaire Breaux," Willoughby announced, pivoting his horse around. "We can get rid of him too, right Matthew?" he queried, nodding his head toward his brother-in-law, who was mounted nearby.

Looking menacing and determined in his brown riding outfit, white hat, and black scarf, Matthew impatiently dismissed Willoughby's remarks. Riding alongside the captain, Matthew shouted, "Now that's enough! Read it!"

The captain fumbled with the scroll, trying to open it. "I said read it!" Matthew shouted again, his family's fortune lending authority to his youth.

"No longer having faith in our juries, mauled as they are by sheriffs who keep away honest men and admit rascals to serve on the jurors' bench, we have formed ourselves into juries!" the captain continued. "You have been found guilty of theft and are condemned to leave this state within two weeks! If you break this bond you will be hanged!"

Pausing long enough to let the impact of his words sink in, the captain shouted, "Let's go!" and the riders began to depart.

Belizaire, still holding Parrain's son protectively, glared up at Matthew on his black horse. Matthew glared back at him, as if to reinforce the warning he had issued Belizaire at his house earlier in the day. The riders took off and the night returned to the silence it had enjoyed before the commotion.

****

Lying on her back in bed under protective mosquito netting, Alida worriedly fingered wisps of her undone hair in the dim lamplight. She heard the door open as Matthew entered as quietly as he could, trying not to wake the children. He stripped off his shirt and pants, tiptoeing up alongside the bed and lifting the netting. Climbing inside, he cuddled up to his wife. Alida turned her face away from him, lying on her side and clutching a pillow. He stretched himself out astride her and kissed her shoulder. He got no response.

"I found Dolsin trying to get into your gun closet today," Alida said in a soft voice.

"He can't get past the lock," Matthew replied confidently, lifting his head from the shoulder he was kissing.

"I know," she said, turning to face him. "But he was trying. He sees you practicing and now he wants to shoot. He needs more of you than that, Matthew."

Matthew knew her anger was not about the gun closet. Touching her hair with one hand and grasping her hand with the other, he said softly, "This vigilante business won't take long."

"And then the slave auctions in New Orleans, the spring roundup? That won't take long either?" she asked as he gently kissed her fingers.

"My father needs me," he replied. She stroked his face with her hand, lightly touching his ears.

"I know," she pleaded, continuing to stroke his cheeks. "But your children, *cher*, your children need you too. And I need you."

He kissed her lightly on the lips and got her attention. He kissed her again and got a response. With an almost desperate longing, Matthew worked his way down to her neck. Her arms twined around his neck, pulling at the back of his head which had buried itself in the softness of her throat. Whispering endearments to him in French, Alida began responding to his passion with her own.

"Sweet . . . my sweet Matthew," she sighed as the need to feel him within her was aroused.

* * * * * * * * * *

In the yard outside Parrain's cabin, a rooster crowed the approaching dawn. Parrain and his wife, Euphemie, sat at their table, and their young daughter Marie was seated in Euphemie's lap. The food she had put out earlier had not been touched. Parrain poured himself a cup of tea while they discussed their plight with Belizaire and Leger.

"We were here longer than they were," Leger protested. "They can't make us go. They can't!"

"But Hypolite," Euphemie replied, shaking her head in exasperation, "The dozen richest men in the parish! What can we do?"

Another young girl, an infant, sat quietly in Leger's lap. Belizaire, sitting next to him, massaged Jean's ankle which was injured trying to fend off the vigilantes. The boy's bandaged face grimaced with pain as Belizaire skillfully manipulated the foot, trying to keep down the swelling and minimize the damage.

"You know what I'm gonna do?" Parrain announced. "Spend the next two weeks smoking as much beef for the trail as I can lay my hands on."

"We won't get hung," Leger insisted. "We can stop them."

"*Puuuu!*" Parrain exploded in disgust.

"Whatever it takes to help, I'll do it," Leger went on.

"Maybe the sheriff will do something," Belizaire put in.

"*Puuuuu-oooo!*" Parrain responded, even more disgustedly than before. "The sheriff? He won't help unless it lines his pockets."

CHAPTER FOUR

The Morning After

It was an angry and frightened group of men who descended on the Vermilion Parish courthouse in Abbeville the morning after they had been visited by the Committee of Vigilance. Eight or nine of them crowded into the front room of the small wooden building, occupying benches or just standing around. The sheriff's waiting room had not been so full since the time two years ago when he had offered a substantial reward for the return of his stolen race horse.

On the front porch were at least as many more men, all chatting worriedly among themselves in French and English about their plight. One man symbolically took his vengeance out on the vigilantes by hitting unwary flies with missiles of tobacco spittle.

"I've been here all my life. They can't tell me to go," a grizzled-looking man in his forties said to an older man sitting on the bench next to him. The older man and several others sitting nearby nodded and voiced agreement with him.

Standing closest to the window facing the street and resting his hand on the sill was Felix Nunez. He stared silently at the others in the room who, like himself, had been ordered to leave the state by the vigilantes the night before.

"Here they come! Here they come!" shouted one of the men outside the building. Everyone in the room fell silent, bracing

Rebecca Perry Willoughby (Nancy Barrett) looks on worriedly from her carriage as her father goes into the courthouse to meet with the sheriff. (Photo by Michael Caffery)

themselves for the confrontation. Theodule Duhon, the young, bearded sheriff's clerk, was the first one outside, followed by the sheriff himself. Dressed in a white shirt, overlapped by a black vest, the gray-haired sheriff had intentionally worn no tie. When soothing ruffled feelings, the respectful formality of a tie often helped, but today actual lives and fortunes would be at stake. It would not pay to be too respectful. A little subtle contempt could enormously improve one's bargaining position.

Escorted by Matthew Perry, Amadee Meaux and several outriders from the vigilantes of the night before, the elaborate barouche carrying Old Perry, his daughter Rebecca, and James Willoughby arrived in front of the courthouse. The slave driving the expensive open-sided wagon halted the horses and Willoughby, dressed in his finest suit and hat, was the first to alight. Old Perry, the gray-bearded patriarch of the parish's largest fortune, climbed slowly off the carriage. He was assisted by his son-in-law Willoughby. Matthew, who accompanied the party on horseback, came over to escort his father.

"Be careful, father," Rebecca warned as Perry began to hobble toward the courthouse. Matthew held onto his arms to support him.

"Stay here with your wife," Perry snapped at Willoughby. "This is no place for a woman."

"Meaux can stay with her," Willoughby replied.

"You stay," Perry snapped again.

Rejection fell over Willoughby's face as he stood and watched Matthew assist the old man up the courthouse steps. Some of the other vigilantes, rifle barrels pointed skyward, formed a protective pocket around him and readied themselves. A showdown with the men they had ordered exiled was very possible, now that they had all gathered and seemed to have the sheriff behind them.

Sosthene Pitre, the crusty old saloonkeeper who had also been ordered into exile, rushed at the sheriff. "When are you going to talk about giving us some protection?" Sosthene demanded.

"Sosthene, you'll get the same kind of protection you always have," the sheriff calmly replied.

"Then I might as well leave for Texas!" Sosthene exploded, throwing his arms in the air and heading for the door.

Perry and his entourage entered the building. Angry words were immediately exchanged. "That's the big man with all his men behind him," one of the exiles sarcastically remarked.

"Out of my way," Perry snapped, rapping the wooden floor with his cane. His men cleared a path through the room for him.

"That's the man that wants to take my land!" Sosthene shouted, pointing an angry finger at Perry.

"Sheriff, throw this man out," Perry growled impatiently.

Heated words filled the air as Theodule firmly ushered Sosthene out of the room. Alighting on the front porch and gesturing contemptuously with his hands, Sosthene repeated his accusations in French before angrily turning to go.

Perry and his group entered the sheriff's office as the sheriff took his place behind his desk. Perry, flanked by Matthew and another vigilante, was seated. The other men stood around behind them, awaiting their audience with the parish's chief law enforcement officer.

"I've called you men in here to save you from getting yourselves into serious trouble," the sheriff began wearily, gesturing as he leaned over his desk toward them. "Twenty families you've exiled. That's too many. Pick five: the five worst. I'll personally see to it that they leave. No need for you gentlemen to dirty your hands."

Perry shook his head. "No sheriff, five is not enough," he said firmly.

"Wait, I wasn't finished," the sheriff went on, sorry but not surprised that his opening offer had been unacceptable. Gesturing with his hands again, the sheriff's voice took on a pleading tone. "You pick five and I'll pick five from that list of twenty you nominated last night with such noise. And those that stay behind will behave or I'll lock 'em up," he concluded, leaning back in his chair.

****

Alida's vegetable garden was surrounded by a crude wooden picket fence. Kneeling down, she carefully inspected the nearly ripe vegetables. Her winter planting had done well. Dressed in a long-sleeved white smock with a long white cap covering her head, she picked the ripest of the plants and placed them in a straw basket she held in her hand.

Hearing a commotion in the yard, she stood and walked toward its source. She heard Dolsin shouting, "Poppa told you never to come back here!"

"Oh, *mon Dieu!*" she exclaimed as she realized the cause of the disturbance. She rushed out of the garden in the direction of her oldest son's cries.

Alongside the barn, Dolsin had Belizaire backed up against the wall, brandishing a sharp, three-pronged pitchfork menacingly at him. Belizaire, confused, had his arms raised to defend himself if need be. He was back as far as he could go against the side of the barn.

"Poppa told you never to come back here!" Dolsin repeated, thrusting the pitchfork toward Belizaire. It was obvious he intended to use it if need be.

Racing onto the scene, Alida grabbed the pitchfork from the boy. "Dolsin, I don't want to ever see you do that again!" she scolded.

"Poppa told him never to come here anymore!" Dolsin protested.

"Go to your room, now!" Alida shouted at him. "Go, Dolsin!"

Like a whipped puppy, Dolsin did as he was ordered, going back to the cabin and ascending halfway up the steps that led to his attic bedroom. Stopping briefly, he turned to look at his mother and Belizaire. "Go!" she shouted and with a long, sad face, he reluctantly climbed the rest of the way up and disappeared into his loft.

"I'm sorry, Belizaire," Alida apologized, leaning the pitchfork against the side of the barn and turning in the direction of the house.

Belizaire shrugged off the incident. "I brought you more citronel," he said, holding a bunch of dried plants out to her like a bouquet of flowers.

"*Merci*," she replied, taking the plants from him. Holding the citronel in one hand and her basket of vegetables in the other, she continued walking toward the house with Belizaire a few steps behind.

"I want to thank you for keeping my secret yesterday," Alida said.

"I am always discreet," Belizaire answered, attempting to keep pace with her.

Stepping onto her front porch, Alida tossed a handful of corn into a crude, hollowed out tree stump that was her pestle and began grinding it with a long wooden mortar. Belizaire followed her as far as the henhouse and stood facing her.

"Was Matthew very angry with you?" Belizaire asked hopefully.

"Matthew gets mad when he's jealous, but it doesn't hurt him to get jealous every now and then, does it?" she asked. She was in good humor, in spite of all that had happened. Belizaire decided that the moment was right to make his move.

"It's not jealousy that makes him and his rich friends terrorize the common people, is it?" Belizaire began, revealing the true purpose of his visit. Walking slowly toward her house, he continued, "Matthew should make his committee realize, Alida, that you, by familial obligation, are still beholden to your own people."

"Belizaire, let's talk about something else. All right?" she replied, continuing to grind her corn.

"Alida, these people are given two weeks. Two weeks to pack up and leave forever," Belizaire said.

"I've heard enough about the vigilantes lately," she answered with obvious annoyance in her voice. "That's it; enough," she pleaded.

"Matthew should make his committee realize . . ." Belizaire persisted, but Alida cut him off.

"Belizaire! Enough!"

She stopped grinding the corn, placing the pole over to the side. Reaching into the pestle, she withdrew the ground meal and briefly inspected it. As she stepped off the porch into the yard, she began calling the chickens to eat.

"Peep, peep, peep. *Vient manger,*" she called out several times, scattering the pulverized corn on the ground. Alida watched as the chickens came scrambling up and began pecking at their food.

Belizaire watched her, clutching the strap of his medicine bag. "Saturday, I play my accordian at the *fais do do,*" he announced. "If they still hold one with all this vigilante trouble," he couldn't help adding.

She looked over and gave him a reproving look. Dismissing the hint he was dropping to her, she went on feeding the chickens as if he hadn't said anything. Belizaire was determined not to let the matter drop quite so easily.

"Oh, Madame Sosthene, bring me Alida," he began singing. "She's the one I have loved since I was fourteen years old." It was an old song that had once been their song. If anything might soften her and bring her over to his side, perhaps the song was it.

Hastily removing his medicine bag and laying it on the ground, he took her hand and swung her around in waltz fashion, while at the same time taking the chicken feed basket from her. She giggled like a girl as he spun her around and continued singing.

"If you don't consent, I will steal her away. She will be mine forever, no matter what you say," he sang.

Belizaire chuckled to himself as he scattered the chicken feed on the ground, Then he became wistful as he addressed Alida again. "You used to come to the *fais-do-do*. You used to be the best dancer on the bayou."

By this time, she was over at the henhouse. Kneeling at the roosts and gathering up eggs, she placed them gently in the long hem of her smock. "No. Not the best," she modestly replied to Belizaire's last flattering remark.

"Then one of the best," he insisted.

"No."

"All of the boys would ask you to dance. We'd watch you as we waited our turn." Each, separately, was becoming caught up in the memory.

Gathering the last of the eggs and holding up the hem of her smock, Alida stood and walked back to where Belizaire was standing. Taking the feed basket from him, she brushed past him and headed up the front steps of the cabin, placing the basket down.

"That was before I met Matthew," she said. It was a denial of the happier, more carefree childhood of which Belizaire was reminding her. Belizaire took the challenge.

"He changed you," Belizaire mused, facing away from her. As he turned and followed her onto the porch, he stooped and picked up the basket, strutting behind her into the house.

"Everybody around here knows he didn't even bother to marry you," Belizaire continued, pressing his point home.

"Belizaire Breaux!" Alida laughed, the tension broken. "You are telling me this?"

"I am," Belizaire replied.

"Well, at least me and Matthew . . . at least we jumped the broomstick," she said, opening the hem of her smock and placing the eggs she held there into a straw-lined basket on a small table in the kitchen. Tying her bonnet further behind her head, she walked toward the window and rinsed her hands in a bowl of water.   Munching slowly on some of the ground corn from the chicken feed basket, Belizaire stared at the woman he loved. A cross dangled from a chain around her neck every time she leaned over. It reminded Belizaire of the sacrament Alida and Matthew had foresaken, and of the opportunity he had missed.

"Jumping the broomstick was fine when there was no church here. But now, with a fine chapel and a real priest, it's inexcusable," he said.

"It was good enough for my grandmother. It's good enough for me," she replied, drying her hands on a nearby cloth.

Still munching thoughtfully on the cornmeal, Belizaire watched her every movement. "If I had a woman like you, I would marry her in a minute. And I'd marry her in the Holy Mother Church," he said earnestly. He meant it. It tormented him that he hadn't said it years ago when it might have made a difference.

As she left the room with the citronel clutched in her hand, Alida brushed past her guest. "If you're going to talk like that, Belizaire, you'll have to leave," she chided him, though in truth, she was not entirely displeased by his remark.

She paused as she entered the living room and stopped in front of her armoire. "But first I'll pay you for yesterday. And today, too," she said.

"There's no charge," he answered.

"I must pay you. These were medical visits. No matter what nonsense you talk," she said, reaching for a sack on top of the armoire.

Moving close enough to make her feel uneasy, Belizaire replied, "I'm not talking nonsense today."

Alida opened the sack, examined the contents, and closed it, pushing it toward him. "Pecans. They're sweet," she said, continuing to thrust the sack at him. "Here. They come from Matthew's poppa's yard."

Belizaire reluctantly took the bag from her and watched as she climbed a chair to hang the citronel from a rope strung between the rafters. Now that it was time to go, he remembered why he had come.

"Maybe you should talk to Matthew about the vigilantes," Belizaire told her. "Have him talk to his poppa."

He saw that his words wounded her. Without waiting for answer, he turned abruptly and was gone.

Climbing down from the chair, Alida walked sadly over to her table and sat down. Brushing her hair off to the side, she stared blankly at the far wall and buried her face in her hands. It was a face that reflected the emotional strain of being on both sides of a divisive issue, one that would give her no peace in the days and weeks to come.

CHAPTER FIVE

The Confrontation

WALKING WITH HIS customary long stride, Belizaire skirted around a pond. His medicine bag was slung low over one shoulder and the sack of pecans given to him by Alida was in his other hand. Ahead of him was a wooden shack thatched with palmetto leaves. Belizaire mounted the two crates which served as steps and entered Sosthene's saloon.

Swinging the crude door toward the inside, he stepped into the dimly lit room. He nodded to Sosthene behind the bar but didn't acknowledge him by any sort of greeting. People enjoyed being rude to Sosthene, though few could match his own rudeness.

"Has Hypolite been by here?" Belizaire asked.

"Tell your cousin Hypolite there's no more credit around here," Sosthene warned in his whiny, high-pitched voice. He was mending an old oxen harness that was stretched out on the bar.

Belizaire's attention was immediately drawn to the three men sitting at a nearby table playing bouree, a popular card game. "Come join the game, Belizaire," one of the card players said. "Hypolite will be by in a while and you will have won enough to pay his bill."

"I do have enough to pay his bill today," Belizaire shot back, tossing the bag of pecans into the air in front of him and catching it. Then, in a single motion, he tossed the bag to the card player

Matthew Perry connects with Belizaire's chin during a fight outside Sosthene Pitre's saloon. (Photo by Michael Caffery)

who spoken to him, and the young man placed the bag in front of an empty chair at the table.

"No more barter," Sosthene whined. "I have to be gone in two weeks."

"Well, maybe we can all start raising chickens again," Belizaire clucked, playfully digging into the crusty bartender's larcenous reputation that resulted in his exile order by the vigilantes.

The other men in the room exploded into laughter. Angry at being made the butt of a joke, Sosthene fussed and griped at Belizaire's comments. "I'm no chicken thief! Why should I steal chickens when there are so many cattle around, anyway?"

Digging in even further, Belizaire fondled some of the items on Sosthene's counter and added, "Since everything that's not nailed down seems to be yours . . ." The other men laughed again, joining Belizaire, who was having the biggest laugh of all. Sosthene went on bad-mouthing Belizaire, but was ignored.

"Deal me in there," Belizaire said, turning his attention to the card players. He hung his hat on a hook behind the table and sat down, pulling the bag of pecans in front of him. Untying the string around it, he took out a few pecans and anted up as a hand was dealt to him.

****

Out at the Perry corral, occupying an enclosed pasture on the edge of the Attakapas prairie, a group of hardened cowhands, some free Cajuns, and some black slaves were branding the calves one by one. It took several men to bring the young animals down and hold them still as the scorching iron branded them with the Perry mark, their bleating protests betraying the discomfort of their ordeal.

The system of branding and registering brands had been taught to the Cajuns by the Spanish. The Americans had learned it from the Cajuns and adopted it also.

As the single-horse carriage bearing Old Perry and Willoughby pulled up, Matthew took a break from the branding to join his father and brother-in-law. Addressing Matthew in his most authoritative voice, Perry said, "You have got to be firmer with these people. This is your plantation, son."

"But what about Rebecca's portion?" Willoughby abruptly put in.

"Matthew will take care of his sister," Perry told his over eager son-in-law. "And he will take care of you, too. Go tend to the cattle, James."

Willoughby turned away and threw up his hands, looking hurt and dejected.

"If it wasn't for him and the vigilante committee, I'd be done with the roundup by now," Matthew told his father.

Willoughby returned, thrusting himself back into the conversation. "I just want to say that if you would take the opportunity . . ."

"James! James!" Perry pleaded, cutting Willoughby off in mid-sentence, not wanting to hear what he had to say. Willoughby persisted.

". . . Take the opportunity . . ." Willoughby tried to continue.

"James! Later! Later!" Perry interrupted again.

"You want me to break that funny-looking nose for you?" Matthew snarled at Willoughby, shaking his finger at him menacingly. There was no disguising the tension that smoldered beneath the surface of their uneasy family relationship.

"You talk brave when you're on the other side of that fence," Willoughby shot back, undaunted by his brother-in-law's threat.

Perry, clearly sensing the tension, gently ushered Willoughby back in the direction of their carriage. He said goodbye to Matthew, who went back to branding cattle. Perry climbed aboard the carriage with Willoughby's help.

"You say you've been running it for ten years?" Perry asked Willoughby as their carriage bumped along the rutted road between ancient live oak and chinaberry trees. Along the way they passed a group of fifteen or twenty field hands on their way to work, their long scythes draped over their shoulders, blades facing backward.

"Your son wants to be an Indian," Willoughby blurted out.
There was no mistaking his desperation to assert his claim to the
patriarch's extensive holdings and bolster his own credentials at
Matthew's expense. "He wants to be a Cajun. That's what he
wants to be; that's his life. He thinks he can make friends with all
these people down here. And at the same time, he thinks they'll
respect him, but he's not one of them and he'll never be."

"James! James! Have you ever thought of shutting up once in a
while?" Perry scolded impatiently. Willoughby roughly snapped
the reins to keep the horse moving forward.

"It'll take someone as strong and hard as you," Willoughby
persisted, determined to press his point home. "I know he's your
son, but Matthew is soft as Louisiana mud."

"But my son will run this plantation," Perry replied emphatically, showing equal determination to see his will carried out.

****

Back at Sosthene's saloon, Belizaire had lost most of the pecans
he brought to gamble with. A mere handful was all that remained
in front of him as the piles of his fellow card players grew in direct
proportion to his losses with each round. Still, Belizaire stayed
with them, hand for hand, determined to compete until he had
won back his share and more.

As they were engrossed in their game, the door was roughly
flung open. In stalked Matthew Perry, his crimson face angrily
contrasting with the expensive camel-colored jacket he wore.
Frightened looks came over the card players as they stared up at
him. Sosthene feigned nonchalance by continuing to mend his
leather and wood harness.

"I told you not to come around my house, Belizaire Breaux!"
Matthew hissed, venting his repressed anger.

"Alida needed medicine, Matthew," Belizaire calmly replied,
leaning back in his chair.

"For what malady?" Matthew demanded, taking a few menacing steps toward the card table. "She doesn't seem sick."

Casting an angry glance at the table, Matthew spied the pecans and recognized them immediately. Belizaire was stalling for time, silently playing with the pecans in front of him. Matthew's tone became even more accusatory.

"I gave those pecans to Alida," he hissed again in Belizaire's direction.

"And she paid me with them," Belizaire answered, keeping calm despite the tension that hung in the air.

"Paid you for what?" Matthew asked. "You aren't even a real doctor! You can't even read and write!"

"I can read some," Belizaire replied, indignant at the accusation.

"Tell me, then, what is her illness? Huh?" Matthew demanded, his voice rising in a steady crescendo.

Belizaire was in a bind. He had promised to keep Alida's pregnancy a secret, yet here was her husband demanding an answer and it was doubtful he would leave without one.

"The female trouble," Belizaire whispered, as if uttering an unspeakable expression.

"The female trouble?" Matthew replied incredulously. "Sounds more like the male trouble to me!" His anger was barely under control.

Determined to put his rival on the defensive and take the heat off himself, Belizaire threw his cards down on the table and stood up slowly. This ploy had to work. "You should be ashamed, Matthew," he began.

"Ashamed of what?" Matthew responded in momentary confusion.

"You come in here and you accuse Alida . . ."

However, Matthew wasn't taken off his guard for long. "I'm not accusing her! I'm accusing you!" he shouted, remembering his purpose for venturing into the hostile establishment.

Belizaire wouldn't let go. "You come here and in front of all these people . . ." he said with a sweep of his hand, indicating the card players and Sosthene. He was playing to the gallery and the gallery was all ears.

"You come and accuse your good, sweet, faithful wife of . .." Belizaire continued, looking both ways before whispering the charge of "infidelity."

"Infidelity?" Matthew asked in disbelief.

"There!" Belizaire announced triumphantly. "He said it again!"

Matthew was so rattled by this time he wasn't sure what he had said. He mumbled a few words that couldn't be understood.

"What are you going do to me, huh?" Belizaire said, challenging him further. "Even your vigilantes, they're not going to do anything to a man as innocent as me."

"Well, I think I might just have you brought before the committee," Matthew threatened, trying hard to get back the upper hand.

Belizaire, ignoring the threat, turned his back on Matthew and started to return to his seat, hoping the issue was resolved.

"No use to bring your vigilantes into this now," Sosthene put in fearfully. "We'll give you back your pecans."

"Non, non!" Belizaire shouted in protest. "Alida gave me those pecans as payment!"

But Matthew liked this solution. He could save face without involving the vigilantes. He had only joined them at his father's insistence anyway.

"Put the pecans back in the sack!" Matthew ordered the other card players.

"I didn't know they were stolen," one of them said. Placing his lit cigar between his lips, he pushed the pecans back into the bag, including the few at Belizaire's seat. Standing by impatiently as his order was carried out, Matthew violently snatched the sack off the table after it was filled and stalked out the door, content with a qualified triumph.

Exiting the saloon with the pecans in his hand, Matthew's heavy range boots carefully sidestepped a mule collar and other assorted junk cluttered around the shaky crates serving as steps to the establishment. Belizaire watched him go, then realized he had missed an opportunity to plead his cousin Hypolite's case. He suddenly rushed after him, shouting "Just a minute, Matthew!" Barreling out the door and tripping over the mule collar, his uncontrolled momentum carried him forward. He fell onto Matthew, knocking him down in the process.

Misinterpreting the accident, Matthew sprang to his feet, his eyes glowering with fury. Seeing his adversary's reaction, Belizaire rolled backward quickly and scrambled to his feet, hoping to escape Matthew's wrath.

"You wanna fight, huh?" Matthew hissed, oblivious to Belizaire's protests of innocence. He lashed out with a right that sailed over Belizaire's ducking head, but a quick follow-up left connected solidly with the medicine man's jaw.

Belizaire was sent flying backward by the impact, crashing through the railing in front of the saloon and hitting the building with his back. He landed heavily on his buttocks at the foot of the wall, dazed but still alert to the danger that confronted him. He got up and away quickly as Matthew charged in desperately.

Dashing off toward a cluster of small trees, Belizaire barely escaped another hard right from Matthew that landed harmlessly an inch or two from the wooden front of the building. Blinded by rage, Matthew pursued Belizaire to the trees where he had taken refuge, deaf to Belizaire's pleas to cease the combat.

"Alida says you are a just man. I believe her," Belizaire pleaded, hoping to calm Matthew down while dodging his frustrated fists. Matthew finally saw an opening and unleashed a crunching right, catching Belizaire on the jaw again, knocking him to the ground. Sosthene and the three card players, peering timorously through the shutters, softly cheered Belizaire on, shaking their fists and rooting for their fellow Cajun's victory.

Warming up to the long-awaited physical showdown with the man he felt was threatening his marriage, Matthew quickly divested himself of his jacket. Belizaire scrambled to his feet and kept a safe distance away, still trying to plead his cause and that of his friends.

"Your committee had no right to exile these people!" Belizaire shouted, as he and Matthew circled each other like two bucks in the woods about to lock horns again.

"I think the committee might have missed one!" Matthew retorted. He and Belizaire continued to circle each other.

"Come on! Come on!" Matthew challenged, gesturing for Belizaire to come forward, still eager to do battle.

"What gives you the right to sentence these people to exile?" Belizaire went on, his voice getting even more indignant while he danced cautiously just out of Matthew's reach.

"We studied each man's past," Matthew replied defensively. It was a question he had asked himself.

"Whose? Whose?" Belizaire demanded as Matthew took another wild swing at him. Skillfully sidestepping the blow, Belizaire caught Matthew's arm and twisted him into a headlock that was more frustrating than painful to the now-helpless American.

"Whose past? Hypolite Leger's?" Belizaire angrily pressed his demand.

"I don't know what you're talkin' about," Matthew protested innocently as he struggled with Belizaire to free himself.

"Hypolite Leger!" Belizaire repeated.

"Huh, what you talkin' about?" Matthew whined. His physical strength was no match for the healer's as he failed to break free of Belizaire's powerful grip around his head and shoulders.

"The fever took his family two years ago. He ran wild for a time, but he is much better now. I would personally guarantee he's better," Belizaire shouted.

"What could your guarantee possibly be worth?" Matthew replied, still frustrated by the hold he couldn't break free of despite his best efforts.

"What is it with you?" Belizaire snarled, shoving Matthew roughly away and propelling him forward with all his might. Matthew crashed heavily into an elevated chicken coop, knocking it over and sending loose feathers and frightened fowl scattering in all directions.

Watching from a window of the saloon, Belizaire's friends cheered the momentary advantage their man had over the hated vigilante.

"Is it because I keep my promise that you are angry?" Belizaire continued, his tirade unabated.

"What promise?" Matthew demanded, brushing himself off and wearily stalking an equally tired, retreating Belizaire. "Huh?" he shouted between heavy breaths, as Belizaire walked away and failed to answer him immediately.

"It's a secret," Belizaire finally replied, walking back toward the saloon.

Matthew was confused and uncertain what to say or do next. What might the secret be, he wondered. Then he remembered the healer's reputation. There was no secret; it was another trick. He caught up with Belizaire and softly placed his hand on his opponent's shoulder. "You and your friend . . . can both go to hell!" he wheezed, slamming a left-handed sucker punch into Belizaire's stomach.

Caught off guard, the wind knocked out of him, Belizaire doubled over and pitched forward onto the dusty ground. Matthew stood over him briefly, grinning in satisfaction at his adversary's pain. His honor satisfied, he turned away, indicating that the bout was over as far as he was concerned.

However, it wasn't over for Belizaire. As Matthew walked toward his horse to retrieve his jacket and the pecans, he turned just in time to see Belizaire charge him like a wild bull. His head caught the pit of Matthew's stomach and Matthew was flung helplessly backward as Belizaire plowed into him.

The two of them splashed into the pond. Struggling to get to their feet in the slimy water while fighting off the mud and duckweed, the plunge seemed to cool their anger as much as it did their weary bodies.

Chuckling smugly as he rose from the shallow muddy water, Matthew made a feint toward Belizaire as if to strike him, but he quickly realized his opponent was beyond his reach. Belizaire wrung out his shoulder-length brown hair, removing strands of duckweed and tossing them back in the water.

"You go ahead and ask her," Belizaire said, taunting Matthew with what he knew. "You ask Alida what the secret is."

"Why would Alida keep a secret from me?" Matthew asked. Maybe it wasn't a trick.

"Because, like many people, she is afraid of your father!"

Matthew paused as the implication slowly sank in. He stared at Belizaire, wondering if he might be telling the truth after concealing it to the point where it almost had to be beaten out of him.

"Yeah, you ask her," Belizaire continued. "Maybe you'll know that I mean you no harm—just as these people here do not deserve your exile!"

For the first time since he had arrived at the saloon, Matthew's voice was something other than hostile and accusatory. He climbed out of the water and let Belizaire's subtle confession register in his confused mind.

"If what you say is true, I'll do what I can for your friend," he promised softly.

Turning to go, he moved toward his horse as Belizaire shouted behind him, "Leger! Hypolite Leger!"

Matthew picked up his jacket and the sack of pecans, repeating the name "Hypolite Leger" to himself. Unexpectedly but gently, he tossed the sack of pecans underhanded to Belizaire, who caught it on the fly.

"You can have the pecans," he said.

Untying the string, Belizaire opened the bag. He took out two of the savory nuts, tied it up again, and tossed the rest back to Matthew.

"I'll take two," Belizaire said, twirling them around in the palm of his hand. "If I lose these, I'll quit playing cards forever."

Sauntering over toward the saloon, knocking the pecans in his hand against each other, Belizaire brushed past Matthew who was now getting ready to mount his horse. "Hypolite Leger," Matthew repeated, slinging his jacket over his shoulder and riding back to his ranch.

Hypolite Leger (Michael Schoeffling) waits for the opportunity to steal a cow from the Perry herd. (Photo by Michael Caffery)

CHAPTER SIX

The Cattle Rustlers

WITH THEIR WHIPS solidly cracking on thick hides and shouts of *"Hippi-ti-yo!"* the young cowboys of the Perry ranch herded in the cattle, aided by some of their Catahoula stock dogs. Led by Amadee Meaux, the mounted ranch hands slowly drove the cattle toward the corrals across the prairie they had been grazing on.

Watching stealthily from behind a huge fallen tree, Hypolite Leger and Parrain hid and awaited their chance to capture one of the strays. "Look how many men they have," Leger whispered fearfully.

"Ssshhh," Parrain whispered back.

Hypolite did not like this at all. He had no qualms about stealing a Perry steer or two, since they had so many and he was sure they would never notice the loss. But the vigilante ride had inflamed everyone's temper. If they were caught in the act, there was no telling what might happen.

Still, he could hardly have refused his help to Parrain. The bonds of blood were too strong.

Willoughby, who had been counting the herd, rode up to Meaux to give him instructions. "Hey Meaux, there's at least six we left in the woods back there. Go get 'em," he said. Meaux promptly wheeled his horse in the direction of the trees.

Taking two other mounted cowboys with him, Meaux went to

round up the stragglers. Matthew came galloping toward Willoughby and circled around him as he reined in his horse.

"Where are they going?" Matthew demanded.

"I sent them for the strays," Willoughby replied.

"I would have gotten to it," Matthew growled, angry over what he perceived as a usurping of his authority.

Willoughby let out a loud sigh of disgust and galloped off, not wanting another confrontation with his over-sensitive brother-in-law.

In the pecan grove where several of the strays were browsing, Leger and Parrain attempted to make off with a stubborn heifer they had lassoed and were leading away. As they struggled with the frightened animal, Meaux spotted them and alerted the other two members of his party.

"Let's get 'em! They're stealing cattle!" he shouted, spurring his horse to a gallop with the other two men following closely behind.

They dashed toward Parrain, who saw them coming and raced off with his horse, abandoning Leger and the stolen cow. All three of the cowboys followed him, leaving Leger and the heifer alone with each other. Leger realized that Parrain needed help. He quickly tied the beast to a tree and shouted, "I'm comin'!" taking off on his own horse to help Parrain.

Lifting his Sharps rifle from the side of his saddle and loading it on the run, Meaux took aim at Parrain. He fired but the shot missed. The sound echoed across the prairie and drew the attention of Willoughby, Matthew, and the other ranch hands. They rushed off in the direction of the shot.

Leger galloped through a row of trees, deliberately drawing the pursuers away from Parrain and onto himself. Turning his posse's attention toward Leger, Meaux fired another shot, missing the young man whose horse was carrying him away from the scene at full speed.

Meaux fired a third shot that missed Leger by only a few feet. The bullet buried itself in the trunk of a tree Leger was rounding. He instinctively ducked as he spurred his horse on.

As the pursuit continued across an open field, Meaux and his men began to bear down on Leger. Two more wild shots were fired as Matthew and Willoughby caught up with the posse.

"Hyahh, yaahh!" Leger shouted to his horse, turning it toward another cluster of trees that would offer him better protection. Pulling up alongside a huge oak tree, Meaux whirled his horse around and propped his rifle carefully across his elbow. Just as he got it level and set his sights on the fleeing Leger, Matthew came up and shoved his arm. The shot went over Leger's head.

"No! No shooting!" Matthew cried.

"You three get after him!" Willoughby ordered.

"No! Let's all get back to the herd!" Matthew said, countering Willoughby's order.

"Matthew . . ." Willoughby pleaded.

"I said no! Let's get back to the herd!" Matthew commanded, making it clear who had the final say on the matter.

Turning away in disgust, Willoughby and Meaux exchanged resentful glances. "That Leger boy, he don't give up, huh?" Meaux said.

"Who?" Matthew asked, overhearing the comment.

"Leger. Hypolite Leger," Meaux answered.

Matthew's expression quickly turned to one of fury on hearing the name of the man he had promised Belizaire he would try to spare from exile. Snapping his reins, he shouted "Come on!" and spurred his horse toward his father's ranch.

****

Standing in Alida's back yard, watching her wash dishes and utensils on a ledge overhanging the kitchen window, Belizaire was shocked to hear about his cousin's theft the day before.

"Who? Hypolite?" he asked in amazement.

"Yes," was her angry reply.

"Nooo," Belizaire said, shaking his head.

"Yes. It was Hypolite," she insisted.

"No, it couldn't have been Hypolite."

"Matthew thinks you two were trying to make a fool of him," Alida shouted, deliberately tossing some of the dirty water from her dishes at him. He jumped back a few steps, but it wasn't enough as some of the water hit him in the face.

"Maybe you think you can make a fool of everybody, Belizaire. You promised not to tell," she shouted accusingly as he wiped his face dry.

"I didn't tell," he protested. "Matthew couldn't beat it out of me."

"Matthew said you started the fight and that you told him to ask me about the baby," she went on, her anger unabated.

"I didn't tell, but an expectant father has a right to know, Alida. But I did not tell."

"Why did you come by, Belizaire, eh? I have enough citronel from you for a month." She began drying the dishes with an old cloth.

"The *fais-do-do* is tonight," he reminded her, his deep, dark eyes penetrating hers.

"Those days are gone," Alida countered, continuing to dry the dishes and utensils more vigorously than before.

"Alida, you could see the neighbors and relatives you hardly see anymore," he pleaded.

"*C'est tout fini*," she replied firmly.

"Why? Is he home tonight?" Belizaire queried.

Alida looked at him as if to say something but didn't. She absent-mindedly went on drying the dishes and began to lapse into a reverie of happier days gone by.

"Alida, you need have no fear for the child you carry," he persisted, abruptly snapping her out of her daydream.

"The baby is not the reason," she replied.

"The unborn, they love to dance," he went on. "I tell you, if it was mine we'd be dancing. And we'd be dancing all the time."

His comment flattered her and, for the first time since his arrival, she let a smile seep through her anger. Shaking her head and giggling softly, she good-naturedly shooed him off.

"Belizaire, home with you. *Va t'en*," she said, motioning toward him with her hands.

His eyes continued to penetrate hers during a long pause that was uncomfortable to her. "Well, it's at Ozeme Guidry's house," he reminded her and went off.

The dreamy look coming back into her eyes, Alida watched him go as she carefully inspected the dishes she had just finished drying.

* * * * * * * * * *

Standing at the edge of a wide, flat prairie, Leger prepared to say goodbye to Parrain and his family. Parrain clutched the reins of a single brown mule hitched to a sledge-like *traneau* that held most of the family's possessions.

"Come with us, Hypolite," Euphemie pleaded as she maternally pressed the infant she was carrying closer to her.

Leger shook his head emphatically. "I don't want to go. I'll be all right," he said.

Parrain handed Leger his revolver. "Here take this, then. You're going to need it," he said.

"What about you?" Leger asked, reluctantly taking the gun from him.

"I got a better one," Parrain replied, snapping the reins and moving the mule forward. Jean walked alongside the mule, guiding it as the *traneau* carried Parrain and his family on the first leg of their long journey to Texas. Behind the vehicle, a rope pulled the heifer Parrain and Leger had captured from the Perry herd.

Holding up his left hand in a gesture of farewell, Leger sadly watched as Parrain and his family crossed the prairie on their way to the new home they were being forced into.

* * * * * * * * * *

As Belizaire approached his cabin on his return from his visit

with Alida, he stopped in his tracks as he heard a suspicious rustling noise inside. Slowly and cautiously making his way up to the
door, he peeked in and saw Leger kneeling on the floor in front of
his armoire, rummaging through it. Leger looked up as Belizaire
entered and guilt crossed his face.

"I know I'm not supposed to dig in your armoire, Belizaire, but
I really needed a drink," Leger said as he stood up.

Belizaire was anything but pleased to see his cousin at that
moment, and he paced toward him angrily. "You rustling Perry's
cattle?" he accused the young man.

"No. Parrain, he needed some meat," Leger answered.

"Matthew Perry was helping you," Belizaire growled, his
anger beginning to rise.

"I didn't know that," Leger said.

"I did this for you!" Belizaire shouted, shaking his finger under
Leger's nose and snatching the small flask of whiskey out of his
hand. He shoved the flask back into his armoire and slammed the
glass door. Then Belizaire poured himself a drink from a jug on the
table, downing it without offering any to Leger.

"Belizaire, we were only after a head or two," Leger protested.

"Where is your Parrain?" Belizaire asked.

"Parrain left for Texas," was the sad reply.

"So what are you doing here?"

"I don't want to go to Texas."

"Get on your horse!" Belizaire ordered.

"No, Belizaire!"

"Right now! Get on your horse and catch up with them. Send
word where you settle and I'll let you know when it's safe to come
back."

Hoofbeats in the yard interrupted them and Belizaire pushed
Leger into a side room. Looking out toward the yard, fearfully
expecting to see Matthew or some of the other vigilantes, Belizaire
was relieved to see a barefoot fifteen-year-old boy on a white horse
carrying a red flag.

"Mr. Belizaire," the boy called as he rode up to the porch.

"What?" Belizaire called back.

"There's a *fais-do-do* at Ozeme Guidry's house tonight!" the boy announced.

"I know that," Belizaire replied. The boy turned his horse and began to ride off.

Belizaire started back inside the house and hesitated, rushing back onto the porch. "Hey wait, T-Paul! *Espere!*" he shouted.

The boy wheeled his horse around and looked back at Belizaire. "Why don't you go by Alida Thibodaux's house?" Belizaire suggested.

"Yes sir," the boy said and continued riding out of Belizaire's yard. Belizaire smiled to himself as he reentered the house.

Belizaire saw that Leger was drinking out of his cup and fondling the accordian with fascination. Belizaire sat down and took another drink. The two of them looked at each other in silence for a few seconds and Belizaire's earlier anger subsided.

"Play," Leger said to him, handing Belizaire the accordian.

Vigilante William Mouton (Bob Edmundson) ties Hypolite to a tree to be horsewhipped. (Photo by Michael Caffery)

CHAPTER SEVEN

Belizaire's Waltz/
Hypolite's Punishment

THE AIR WAS festive and lively at Ozeme Guidry's house where the *fais-do-do* was being held. Cajun men, women, and children from miles around had come to dance, eat, drink and take a break from their otherwise harsh lives.

In the living room, all the tables and chairs had been moved to the side. Half a dozen couples were dancing a two-step to the music provided by two fiddlers, a triangle player, and Belizaire who was playing his accordian. Many of those not dancing were standing around the perimeter of the room, clapping along, nodding their heads in time with the music, or whooping it up. The whining yet melodic voice of a man crooned the song in French.

Mrs. Guidry, wearing her long brown dress, scattered corn starch on the floor, making it easier for the dancers to move across the cypress planks. Families were warmly greeted by the hosts and others on their arrival. Their children hungrily eyed the cakes, tarts, soft drinks, and other treats laid out on a table along the wall. Some of those who had arrived earlier and settled in were spooning gumbo from wooden bowls into their mouths. Others were cracking open the crawfish boiled up for the occasion and sucking the meat from the tails.

At a side table, a group of men were playing cards and nodding subconsciously along with the music. Groups of women sat on benches along the edge of the room, gossiping and fanning themselves. A dozen or more married couples sat together, resting from previous dances and waiting for the next number to begin.

Some of the younger children, tired out at the end of a long day, were brought to an attic bedroom where seven or eight little ones were already asleep on a bed. Others dozed on cushions and blankets on the floor. Their mothers, intent on having a good time, left their young ones in the room with a final parting order for them to go "*do-do*," the Cajun expression for sleep.

In the middle of the living room floor, wedged between other couples, Leger danced with a serious-looking fifteen-year-old girl, her dark hair pulled up under a white *snood*. As Leger moved her slowly back and forth, the girl glanced apprehensively at the floor, watching their feet. Leger, clad in his favorite rust-colored shirt, was drunk and he moved unsteadily to the rhythm.

The song ended, with Belizaire holding the final note on the accordian for a few extra seconds. As the partygoers clapped and cheered the musicians, Leger let go of the girl's hand and they bowed their heads slightly toward one another.

"Thank you. You dance real good," Leger said.

"You're welcome," she replied without any emotion. Hustling over to the side of the room, obviously eager to be rid of him, she added politely "I enjoyed it too."

Leger watched her for a few seconds as she ran over to her mother, who was cooling herself off with a palmetto fan. Just as he turned to go, the girl sat down and held her foot up to her mother.

"Mama, I think he broke some of my toes," she whined as her mother carefully inspected them.

Leger stepped onto the porch in the bright lamplight. He was handed a wine jug by Sosthene who had been guarding it as if it were gold bullion. With Sosthene were four or five other men, mostly around his age, drinking and smoking their corncob pipes while reclining in wicker rocking chairs. Leger looped the small handle of the bottle with his right index finger and lifted it to his mouth, taking a long swig.

"Take it easy, Hypolite," Sosthene warned in his high-pitched voice, tapping Leger on the rear end. "You've had a lot already and you're in trouble, boy."

Leger lowered the jug and handed it back to Sosthene, wiping his mouth with the side of his hand.

Suddenly the eyes of all the men on the porch turned toward the shadowy figures of a woman and her children approaching the front gate. Then they saw it was Alida. She entered the Guidrys' yard carrying Aspasie, trailed by Valsin and Dolsin. There was a momentary pause in their conversation as the surprise registered. She hadn't been to a *fais-do-do* or any of their other functions in ten years. Sosthene spoke first and the words of greeting he chose were not the most flattering.

"Well, it's Alida and her three *half-Americains*," he whined bitterly. "You come to say goodbye to the people your husband is sending away?"

Alida was dressed in a white blouse and ankle-length beige skirt. Her long brown hair trailed down her back, held in place by two barrettes. She looked more radiant than she had in quite some time.

Approaching the house with her flock, she ignored the old saloonkeeper's remarks and walked up to Leger. In a soft, sad voice, she expressed her regrets over his exile order by the vigilantes and ended by saying, "I'm sorry."

Leger, head hung low, uttered "I don't want no trouble with you," and walked around her suspiciously. He reentered the house ahead of Alida and her children.

"Ever been to Texas, son?" Sosthene asked Dolsin, getting in one last jab as the boy was about to step inside. Dolsin looked at him and said nothing as he followed Alida and Valsin into the Guidry home. Sosthene chuckled and shrugged his shoulders, taking another swig from his jug.

As Alida entered the room, everyone turned to look at her and the children. Her unexpected appearance stunned some of them into momentary silence. However, after the few seconds of disbelief wore off, long-lost friends came up and welcomed her, looking in amazement at the children and commenting on how big they had gotten since they had seen them last. Alida glanced around the room and smiled at the music and dancing, memories of a happier youth coming back to her very quickly.

Leger was now more intoxicated than he had been earlier. He weaved unsteadily across the dance floor, sidestepping the waltzing couples, as he made his way toward the girl he had danced with earlier. He saw her sitting on the side of the room and staggered over, holding out his hand and asking her to dance with him.

"I don't want to," the girl said emphatically, remaining in her seat.

"Come dance with me again," he said, taking her hand and roughly yanking her up.

"I don't want to," she repeated, pulling away from him.

"Come on!" he demanded brusquely, still tugging violently on her arm.

"I don't want to!" she screamed, jerking free of him and backing up into her seat.

Her outburst startled many people in the room, including Belizaire and the other musicians. People glared at the drunken Leger, who wasn't sure what to do next. The young girl, embarrassed to be the object of so much attention, ran from the room. Her mother followed.

"He insulted my daughter!" shouted a burly man in a blue shirt as he came rushing out of the kitchen toward Leger.

Ozeme Guidry, himself a large, powerful man, quickly hustled over to take charge of the situation. "I know. I know," he reassured the girl's angry father. "It's my house. I'll take care of this."

"Hypolite!" Guidry called out, marching toward Leger.

"Uh oh," Leger muttered as he saw the two big men bearing down quickly on him.

"You're going to have to leave, Hypolite," Guidry quietly commanded.

"Leave?" Leger responded, misunderstanding the host's order and acting surprised. "You're not a vigilante."

"I know, but it's my house," Guidry went on firmly, tapping his heart with the palm of his left hand. "You know I let anybody come here but I have two rules: the drinks stay outside and the drunks stay outside."

Sensing trouble, Belizaire unstrapped his accordian and made his way toward the tense scene. "Now go with Belizaire," Guidry quietly ordered Leger.

"I'm not going to go," Leger replied with equal firmness.

On hearing this, the girl's father pushed Guidry aside and rushed at Leger with his fists cocked. Belizaire planted himself between the prospective combatants, and quickly grabbed the angry man, shoving him back and preventing him from hitting Leger. The man grappled with Belizaire, trying to get at Leger, but Belizaire's strength and his determination to prevent further trouble prevailed.

"You're not a vigilante, are you?" Leger protested. "I ain't leavin'!"

Belizaire continued to struggle with the girl's father, who was still shouting, "He insulted my daughter!"

"Wait!" Guidry pleaded, "Belizaire'll take care of him!"

Acting quickly to protect his hot-headed young cousin, Belizaire shoved Leger through the curtain that separated the room from the porch, getting him out of the angry father's reach. Alida and the others in the room watched fearfully as the shouting and shoving match went on. Finally, Belizaire got Leger off the battlefield and the festive atmosphere was restored. The band, minus Belizaire, struck up again and couples went back to dancing as if nothing had happened.

"I'm not going! I ain't gonna go!" Leger's shouts could be heard from outside as Belizaire escorted him toward his horse. Leger leaned drunkenly on Belizaire, whose arm was firmly around his shoulders.

"I feel sick," Leger moaned.

Belizaire didn't answer, but lifted Leger's left foot into the stirrup of his white horse. Giving a mighty heave, Belizaire hoisted Leger into the saddle, where he flopped over, groping for the other stirrup with his right foot.

"I feel bad," Leger groaned.

"Well, then you go to my house and go to sleep right now," Belizaire said, placing Leger's hat on his head.

"I'm afraid of Texas, Belizaire," Leger whimpered, adjusting the hat up over his eyes. "Are things going to be all right?"

"I don't know," was Belizaire's soft reply.

"But you know everything."

"No, I don't know everything."

"You always said you did."

Belizaire paused thoughtfully, smiling gently and rubbing his beard. "Yeah, well I guess I meant almost everything. Come on, go to my house and go to sleep, huh," he said.

"Good night, Belizaire," Leger whispered, nearly in tears. He prodded the horse and it carried him slowly through a glade leading into the woods. Moved by his young kinsman's plight, Belizaire sadly watched Leger ride off, his lanky body swaying unsteadily in the saddle. Convinced that Leger would be all right, he turned and headed back to the Guidry cabin and the lively sounds of the dance still going on inside.

From the top step of the porch, Belizaire took one last glance at the wobbly Leger riding off through the trees. "Don't worry, Belizaire," one of the old men sitting on the porch said to him. "His horse will get him home."

"Home? It'll get him all the way to Texas," Sosthene chimed in bitterly.

Belizaire turned toward Sosthene and the four other older men who sat around drinking Sosthene's wine, while they rocked and smoked their pipes. He plopped down on the edge of the porch and asked Sosthene to pass him the wine. Handing the jug to a heavy-set bearded man sitting next to him, Sosthene told the man in French to pass the jug to Belizaire.

"You made that?" Belizaire asked the crusty saloonkeeper,

carefully inspecting the jug before taking a drink from it.

"Yup. Sure did," Sosthene replied proudly. "There's much more where that came from."

"Yeah, you always made the best wine, Sosthene," Belizaire said, taking a swig and smacking his lower lip. "We're sure gonna miss it after you've gone to Texas."

He broke out into a laugh and the other men on the porch joined in. Sosthene, who hated being made fun of, cursed at them.

* * * * * * * * * *

Riding through a grove of verdant trees, his slumped form silhouetted in the bright moonlight, Leger continued to sway in the saddle of his slow-moving horse, humming a tune that was off-key. Suddenly, unable to hold on any longer, he slipped from the saddle and fell heavily to the ground on his back.

Without a rider to guide it, the horse stopped abruptly and Leger pulled himself up with a groan, yanking on the stirrup for support. Unable to get himself into the saddle, however, Leger spun the horse around and fell again, this time frightening it away.

"I'm sorry," he called out pitifully to the horse as it ran off through the woods. Groaning and struggling to his feet, he bent over a bush and threw up.

* * * * * * * * * *

Back at the Guidry house, Belizaire seized his long-awaited opportunity and waltzed gracefully with Alida the full length of the floor and back. She smiled and showed every indication of having a good time.

Belizaire's fixed expression was one of deep, supressed, yet undisguised love. He held her hands as if they were precious gems and they floated around the room to the rhythmic bayou music they had grown up with. For Alida, it had been a long time since she'd had so much fun, and she was determined to savor every minute of it.

****

Staggering through the slowly darkening woods, whistling and calling his horse, Leger stumbled over exposed tree roots as he groped his uncertain way toward Belizaire's house. The music of the *fais-do-do* in the distance was still audible, but it was getting faint.

"Oh no!" Leger gasped, glancing fearfully over to the side of him. He broke into a run, but he still wasn't fast enough to escape the small group of vigilantes who waited in the shadows on foot and on horseback to waylay him.

"Get him!" a voice cried as Leger staggered away from them. Powerful arms subdued him, wrestling him to the ground. Leger struggled against the men holding him and attempted to take a swing at the nearest of them, but his arm was pinned. A rope was quickly looped around him and pulled taut. Overpowered and screaming in vain, Leger was dragged helplessly toward the trunk of a nearby oak tree.

One by one, lanterns were lit and Leger recognized the faces of Willoughby, Matthew, Meaux, and the others who had ordered him into exile several nights earlier. "Let me go! Leave me alone!" he cried, but the vigilantes were deaf to his pleas.

With Willoughby supervising, Leger was stripped of his shirt, which was pulled loosely in front of him over his arms. One of the vigilantes menacingly slapped the butt of a whip against the palm of his hand as another pulled the rope that held Leger tighter around the tree trunk.

"Tie him up! Get him up here!" Willoughby ordered.

Meaux roughly shoved Leger closer to the tree as the rope around him was painfully tightened.

Stepping forward authoritatively, Matthew pushed Meaux aside and placed his hand gently on Leger's head, inspecting the young man's condition. "Let him go," he softly commanded.

"What's the matter? Did he hurt him?" Willoughby interjected sarcastically.

"That man is drunk. He doesn't even know what's happening," Matthew remarked, removing his hand from Leger's head. "There's no whipping that's needed here," he concluded, walking away.

"You gonna let him go again?" Willoughby shouted.

"There's no whipping that's needed, I said. Let's take him down from the tree," Matthew ordered.

"Matthew shouldn't have to do it if he's too soft," Willoughby said, ignoring Matthew's order. "Let Meaux do it. Here get the whip."

One of the vigilantes passed the whip toward Meaux. Matthew snatched it out of his hand, an action that provoked a heated confrontation with Willoughby. The two antagonistic in-laws squared off face to face, their jutting jaws only inches apart.

"What! You gonna let him go again?" Willoughby snarled. "Why don't you let the man whip him? Then you can kiss it and make it better! Isn't that what you want?"

"You know what I wish?" Matthew hissed, meeting Willoughby's sarcasm head on.

"You'd make him feel better, wouldn't you?" Willoughby shot back.

"You know what I wish?" Matthew repeated.

"Then he'd be pussy-whipped like you are!" Willoughby taunted.

"I wish it was you tied to that tree!" Matthew said, finally finishing the sentence.

Matthew gazed sadly at the whip in his hand. Reluctantly he raised it, preparing to administer the punishment. He knew it was better that he should do it instead of Meaux, who might kill Leger just for the sport of it. Satisfied that he had goaded Matthew into performing the deed, Willoughby smiled at Meaux and joined him over on the side to witness Leger's punishment.

The lash whistled over Matthew's head and cracked on Leger's bare back, opening an ugly gash from his left armpit almost to his neck. Leger screamed in agony. He struggled vainly against the bonds holding him to the tree.

Matthew struck him again, and a third time, then a fourth, each blow landing more painfully than the one before it. Bloody streaks criss-crossed the young Cajun's back. He slumped toward the ground, held up by the ropes which strained against his wrists and cut off his circulation. After the fifth blow, Leger began screaming threats at his tormentor.

"Matthew Perry, I'm gonna kill you!" Leger shouted in his agony.

Matthew continued to deliver the punishment, wielding the whip sideways from his waist. "I'm gonna kill you! I'm gonna kill you!" Leger continued to scream with each painful lash.

Willoughby, Meaux, and the other vigilantes glanced at each other from the sidelines. They were nervous about their lawless actions, but they were also satisfied that justice as they perceived it was finally being carried out. Leger's screams echoed through the still, hot air, transforming what had already been a bad evening for him into a living nightmare.

****

Unaware of the terror his troublesome cousin was suffering, Belizaire was back on his accordian playing a lively contradanse along with the other musicians. He was smiling and never took his eyes off Alida as she pranced around the floor in a circle with another bearded man. As the last note was struck, the man spun Alida around twice and she laughed softly. They bowed their heads toward one another and made their way off the floor amid the cheering and clapping of the crowd.

In the brief silence between numbers, Belizaire suddenly cocked his ear toward the open window as a cry in the distance caught his attention. Several others in the crowd also heard it, and an apprehensive hubbub went up among them.

"*Les vigilantes!*" a fearful voice said, barely above a whisper.

"Ssshhh! Be still!" Belizaire ordered.

Leger's painful cry was heard again, and nearly everyone in the room gasped. Thrusting his accordian toward a man standing behind him, Belizaire sprang up and raced out the front door.

A crowd trailed him onto the porch and into the yard. Belizaire grabbed a lantern and stopped by the gate as he heard still another cry. Nervous voices buzzed in the crowd, and Alida clutched her breast in anguish, watching Belizaire venture off toward the woods.

"We should stop them," said one of the men on the porch, keeping a safe distance behind Belizaire.

"Yeah, then we could all go to Texas together," Sosthene whined sarcastically. "Make a wagon train."

Another buzz went through the crowd at Sosthene's frightful reminder of the sentence pronounced by the vigilantes on some of them. They turned and passively walked back toward the house.

"I don't want any part of this," said the father of the girl Leger had danced with earlier. Several other voices in the crowd agreed.

"Yeah, we got our families to think of," Guidry said.

The crowd dissolved and most of them went back inside, leaving Belizaire to face the danger alone. Gingerly approaching the woods, fearful for his safety but determined to help his kinsman, he ventured into the darkness, his lantern guiding him along the way.

As he reached a clearing, Belizaire heard heavy, painful breathing and directed his attention toward the ground in front of him. He knelt down and placed the lantern in front of him, solemnly examining the stretched-out body of Leger, his back torn to shreds by the whipping Matthew had given him.

Lying face down on the damp earth, Leger's labored breathing gave Belizaire some measure of relief as he placed his ear close to his cousin's head and chest. As he stooped over Leger, a doctor examining his patient, Belizaire nodded his head in satisfaction, knowing the young man was still alive.

Standing up and remembering a spider web he had seen nearby, Belizaire took up a stick and knocked the spider off its home. He severed the branch from the rest of the tree and brought the sticky web over to Leger, applying it to his wounds. Patiently and carefully, with practiced hands, Belizaire stretched the spider web to its fullest elasticity and managed to cover nearly all of Leger's injuries with it.

"It hurts," Leger whimpered softly, lifting his head. "It hurts bad, Belizaire."

Cradling his cousin's head gently, Belizaire held him for a few seconds. His strong, wordless compassion reassured Leger that he had at least one friend left in a world that had suddenly turned against him.

****

The next day at dawn, Belizaire stalked up to Alida's cabin, his eyes glowing with fury. He slammed his fist four or five times on a shutter that covered her bedroom window. "Matthew! Come on out here!" he shouted.

The shutter opened slightly and Alida, in her night clothes, peered out fearfully. "Quiet, Belizaire. You'll wake the whole house," she whispered.

"I want to talk to Matthew!" he demanded angrily.

"He's not home now. You can't talk to him," she replied, trying to calm him down.

"Who is he whipping now!" Belizaire accused as he walked around to the porch and climbed onto it. Leaning against the wall, he said, "I'll wait."

Alida closed the shutter and seconds later appeared at the front door, standing nervously across the threshhold. Her long brown hair hung in unruly strands over her shoulders. She clutched at her breasts apprehensively as she gazed at Belizaire leaning against the wall, clearly targeting himself for trouble should Matthew appear.

"You come away with me, Alida!" Belizaire desperately pleaded. "You come away from this place with me right now!"

"I can't. I can't. I'm a married woman," Alida sadly replied.

"Not in the eyes of my God. No! You are not a married woman!" he countered, his voice rising in proportion to his anger.

"I am. Even if there is no paper to say so, I am," she defensively responded. Patting her heart, she said, "I have Matthew," and patting her belly, she added, "and I have my children. There's no place left for you, Belizaire."

"No! Matthew has his father and his vigilantes and there is no room left for you!" Belizaire replied.

"It's too late. It's too late. Please, Belizaire, you must leave before Matthew returns. Please," she implored him, gesturing in desperation with her hands.

He remained unmoved by her protests of fidelity to a marriage their Catholic faith deemed unconsecrated. "My God, I could love you if you come away from this place with me right now," he pleaded.

"And what about my children?" she demanded, crossing angrily over the porch toward him. "How are you going feed my babies? With pecans you can't even keep?"

Her face, flushed with anger, was only inches from his. He fell silent, but his penetrating eyes took in the beauty of her hardened, dark features. He was enjoying the closeness of her body despite her annoyance at his unwanted intrusion into her domestic life.

"What do you have to offer us, Belizaire?" she raged on, waving her hands animatedly at him. "What can you give us? Dolsin, he wants a horse for his birthday! Where would you ever get him a horse? Where would we go? Where would you take us?"

Continuing his penetrating stare for a few more seconds, Belizaire reluctantly acknowledged his defeat. She was right and he knew it. His head bowed low in sorrow, he turned to go. Walking sadly off the porch, he crossed the yard without so much as a backward glance at her.

Alida watched until he had disappeared from view. A shuffling noise in the attic distracted her, and she turned her head to see an eavesdropping Dolsin scurrying back into his bedroom loft. She started to scold him, but held off. Instead she gazed after Belizaire, her face etched with even more anguish than it had borne before.

Academy Award winner Robert Duvall, appearing in a cameo role, plays the part of a preacher at Matthew Perry's funeral. Duvall was a creative advisor to the film and his wife, Gail Youngs, played the lead female role. (Photo by Michael Caffery)

CHAPTER EIGHT

"... The Lord Gave,
the Lord Hath Taken Away ..."

MATTHEW'S FAILURE TO return home that night had Alida and the children worried. She had long since gotten used to his late meetings of the Committee of Vigilance and the rides they took to enforce their decrees, but never had he stayed out the entire night.

The mystery of his disappearance didn't take long to unravel. The following day, as a group of women were washing their clothes alongside the bayou, one of them looked up and saw Matthew's body floating face up in the shallow water. She let out a frightened gasp, loud enough to draw the attention of the other women. One of them ran to the village to fetch help.

A group of men came running over, and several of them waded into the water to retrieve the body. Matthew's waterlogged corpse was pulled ashore, the blood from the bullet wound in his heart still visible though most of it had washed away. The men shook their heads sadly as they lifted the body onto a wagon hitched to three horses.

By this time, Alida had been informed of the tragedy by a fast rider racing ahead. When she heard the news she did not believe it. Before she ran to meet the procession, she told her children to stay, but Dolsin followed anyway. She dashed toward the wagon, crying hysterically, with Dolsin close behind her. They jumped over the railing and Alida flung herself on the shroud covering her dead husband, peeling it back and wailing frantically.

"Matthew! Matthew! No! No!" she cried touching his face and moving his limp head from side to side. Still in shock, she hugged and shook him, rocking back and forth with him and crying. Shaking him by the shoulders, tears streaming down her panic-stricken face, she let out a piercing scream and fell forward on top of him.

Dolsin stood over her in dry-eyed silence, his youthful face haunted by the sight of his father's dead body.

The driver shouted to the horses and snapped the reins, steering the wagon toward town. Alida remained on board, crying and wailing and hugging Matthew's body in desperation.

As the wagon passed along the main street in Abbeville, townspeople walked and trotted behind it curiously, gazing silently at the body and the grief-stricken young widow. Other villagers, standing solemnly on their porches as the wagon passed, bowed their heads in respect and closed their doors and shutters, observing an ancient French custom for the dead. Some of them attempted to console Alida but she was still too shocked to acknowledge their sympathy.

The driver pulled the wagon to a halt in front of the courthouse. The sheriff solemnly came outside with his chief deputy Theodule behind him. Climbing onto the wagon bed while Theodule waited on the ground nearby, the sheriff gently attempted to pull Alida off Matthew's body so he could begin his inquest. Alida, still frozen with terror, refused to let go despite the sheriff's efforts to move her.

"No! No! Please! Matthew!" Alida screamed as the sheriff finally succeeded in breaking her grip on the corpse. Still crying, Alida was helped down from the wagon by some of the townspeople. The sheriff and Theodule grimly inspected the crimson wound in Matthew's heart, looking for clues in the murder.

It wasn't until late afternoon that the sheriff concluded his investigation and released the body to Matthew's family. After he had filed his report, the same wagon that had brought the body into town took off in the direction of the Perry ranch. Alida and the children, ostracized by Old Perry, went to stay with her own family and friends.

The wagon arrived at the Perry plantation and pulled up a a short distance from the main house. Willoughby and Meaux, accompanied by several ranch hands and slaves, went up to the vehicle and gently removed Matthew's body, carrying it toward the house. From the balcony, the elder Perry looked on in silent shock, held up by Rebecca and an elderly black house servant named Jonathan. Perry's face reflected the horror that had just begun to register over the tragic death of his only son.

Nearby, a group of slaves stood in silent respect, removing their hats and leaning on the tools they were using to prepare a garden. A cloud of gloom hung over the estate as Matthew Perry was brought home for his final rest.

****

Leger, his back heavily bandaged to cover the wounds he had received the night before, limped out of Belizaire's cabin leaning on the older man's shoulders. In the yard, Leger's horse was saddled and ready to carry him off.

"Listen," Belizaire cautioned him, "They'll expect you to go west. Go south instead to Cheniere au Tigre."

"No!" Leger protested.

"That's where you'll catch a schooner, Hypolite, and you'll sail on to Galveston," Belizaire went on, helping Leger onto his horse.

"But Parrain . . ." Leger continued to protest.

"Your Parrain got you into this!" Belizaire shouted, losing patience with Leger's stubbornness. "Now do as I say and go!"

Leger held his peace and made no attempt to argue further. As he sat erect and sober in the saddle, Belizaire reached up and cut off a lock of Leger's hair with a knife.

"I will pray for you," Belizaire said sadly.

"I'll miss you," Leger replied sadly. He started to cry as he looked down at the cousin he was leaving behind in his exile.

Belizaire slapped the horse's rear end and shouted, "Hyaahhh!" The horse took off at a gallop, scattering goats and chickens throughout the yard. Watching him go in sad silence, Belizaire gestured farewell to the young man who'd been almost like a son to him. He crossed himself and watched as Leger finally disappeared from view.

* * * * * * * * * *

On the day of Matthew's funeral, nearly the entire population of Vermilion Parish turned out, either to pay their respects or simply to gaze on in curiosity. The differences in the class structure between the landowners and the poorer Cajun bayou folk were clearly evident. The well-to-do stood on the inside of the fence surrounding the graveyard, while the poorer residents lined the outside perimeter of it.

"I will praise thee with my whole heart: before the gods will I send praise unto thee," the balding minister recited at the graveside, looking down and reading scriptures from his Bible. "Whither shall I go from thy spirit or whither shall I flee from thy presence?" he droned on against the sound of women softly weeping.

Vigilantes, their rifles poised upward, in readiness, lined the inside of the fence about twenty feet apart to prevent any possible trouble. Their job that day was to keep the Cajuns on "their side" of the fence and in their place while the elite, dressed in their finest mourning clothes, paid their final respects.

"If I ascend up into heaven, thou art there," the preacher went on. "If I make my bed in hell, behold, thou art there. If I take the wings of the morning and dwell in the uttermost parts of the sea; even there shall thy hand lead me, and thy right hand shall hold me. Naked came I out of my mother's womb, and naked shall I return thither: the Lord gave and the Lord hath taken away; blessed be the name of the Lord."

Outside the fence, surrounded by her friends and family, Alida clutched Aspasie in her arms. Dressed entirely in black and her face covered by a thin black veil, she sobbed softly as the graveside service went on for the husband whose family would not allow her to share the grief alongside them. Dolsin, his hat draped over his eyes and his face dry but torn with anguish, stood by in silence. Next to him was Valsin and all around them were aunts, uncles, and other relatives from Alida's family.

"Therefore are they before the throne of God, and serve him day and night in his temple: and he that sitteth upon the throne shall dwell among them," the preacher continued, as Willoughby, Meaux, and four other black-garbed pallbearers carried Matthew's plain wooden casket on ropes suspended underneath it. Passing over the hole in the earth, three on each side of it, they slowly lowered the casket until it came to rest on the soft mud at the bottom.

"They shall hunger no more, neither thirst anymore; neither shall the sun light on them, nor any heat," the service continued as the sheriff and Theodule looked on. "For the Lamb which is in the midst of the throne shall feed them, and shall lead them unto living fountains of waters: and God shall wipe away all tears from their eyes." Alida and her children stared straight ahead, straining to catch a glimpse of Matthew's grave.

Standing a short distance away from Alida and her mourning family, Belizaire also looked on solemnly, leaning on a fencepost. Alongside him, Sosthene also wore a serious expresssion but it didn't appear to be genuine, as he witnessed the funeral of a vigilante ringleader who had sentenced him into exile from his beloved bayou home. It was an expression of satisfaction more than anything else.

As the funeral went on, Willoughby and Meaux looked at each other apprehensively as if they shared a secret. Behind them, Old Perry leaned on his cane, his feeble body looking as if it would collapse under his anguish. Rebecca held him up by one arm, weeping softly while Jonathan held the other arm as the service began to conclude.

"Jesus said . . . 'I am the ressurection, and the life: he that believeth in me, though he were dead, yet shall he live: and whosoever liveth and believeth in me shall never die. Believest thou this. Amen,'' the pastor whispered, lifting his thumb from the pages and allowing the breeze to ruffle them. Slowly closing the the Bible, his head still bowed in reverence, he looked up only after the other mourners had repeated "Amen." Placing his wide-brimmed black hat on his balding head, the preacher made one final gesture toward the grave and departed. Several of the vigilantes followed him.

William Mouton, a large, red-bearded vigilante walking a few steps behind the preacher came up to another armed man and told him softly, "We're gonna ride!" The other man nodded and said nothing.

The mourners began to leave the cemetery. After casting a few flowers into the open grave, the Perry party made its way off, followed by friends of the family. Women clutching the arms of their husbands, their children in tow, pulled their veils more tightly around their faces as they walked away. The men placed their hats back on their heads. The gravediggers finished their work of covering up the hole.

Outside the fence, the townspeople had already begun to depart. With a silent nod toward Belizaire, Sosthene made his way off. Belizaire, however, remained on the scene, his eyes fixed on Alida and her family. He was uncertain what to do next.

Surrounded by her family, Alida accepted their final condolences. She left the two youngest children in the custody of three of her aunts, and kissed them goodbye. Two of the aunts held Valsin's hands and another held Aspasie in her arms as they walked away. With a black wreath in one hand and her other arm draped over Dolsin's shoulders, Alida slowly made her way into the graveyard after all the other mourners had left. A few more townspeople stopped to offer their sympathies and she nodded to them as she went solemnly about her mission.

Belizaire remained frozen to the fencepost, fighting off an urge to go up to her and offer what consolation he could. He watched sullenly as she and Dolsin knelt reverently before Matthew's still open grave, laying the black wreath on it and uttering silent prayers as they paid their final respects to their loved one.

Walking away from the cemetery, the sheriff overtook Perry and his party as they neared their carriages. Lightly grasping one of the old man's frail arms, the sheriff assisted Jonathan in keeping Perry erect.

"If this keeps on, there'll be no stopping it," the sheriff warned, referring to the vigilante activity. "It won't stop."

Perry, still overcome with grief, didn't answer. Willoughby was a few steps behind them, escorting Rebecca, and he strained to hear the sheriff's words. Rebecca's head turned back toward the grave, and she stopped as she saw Alida and Dolsin kneeling there. Her face reflected sympathy toward the young widow and her family, but Willoughby tugged on her arm directing her forward.

As Willoughby and Jonathan helped Perry onto his barouche, Belizaire approached them, hoping to smoothe out a volatile situation. "Monsieur Perry, I'm sorry!" he said, attempting to be conciliatory. He moved closer to the wagon, but Willoughby looked at him with undisguised contempt.

"Look, I beg you to hear me," Belizaire continued. "How could a man do harm, let alone take the life of another man if he could not walk?"

"Stay away from here!" Willoughby growled, climbing onto the side of the barouche as Belizaire got closer.

"After the whipping these men gave Hipolyte Leger, he could not walk," Belizaire pleaded.

"Show some respect!" Willoughby growled again, roughly shoving Belizaire away with his foot. Belizaire sprawled backward to the ground and Willoughby dismounted, preparing to get even more physical if the occasion warranted it. He glared at Belizaire for a few seconds before shouting "Get 'em out!" and the carriage took off down the road. Willoughby waved goodbye to his wife and father-in-law, and walked over to the group of vigilantes who were preparing to ride.

From the barouche, Perry never looked back at Belizaire nor did he acknowledge his pleas in any way. Rebecca looked back apprehensively. She seemed to want to do something but her fear of Willoughby prevented her from doing anything.

Undaunted by Willoughby, Belizaire jumped up, dusted himself off, and raced after the departing carriage. "I tied his wounds!" Belizaire shouted, still pleading Leger's cause to the old man.

"Listen, Matthew's children—you've got to provide for them now!" Belizaire went on, running after the barouche. "They'll need milk . . . and rice. They're just babies. Monsieur Perry! Monsieur Perry, please?"

Sensing the futility of his pleas, Belizaire finally gave up and sadly watched the carriage move along the road. Turning his attention elsewhere, Belizaire headed over toward the vigilantes who were saddling up their horses in defiance of the sheriff's warnings.

"You better get these men off these horses," the sheriff warned Willoughby. "They'll be criminals. If you men touch one hair on that boy's head, I'll jail the whole lot of you. You puttin' yourselves above the law."

Willoughby and the other vigilantes ignored him. Moving closer to Meaux, Willoughby heard his companion say he was taking the men by the Cypress Island road.

"Make sure you get him!" Willoughby whispered.

"I know that Leger boy," Meaux replied confidently.

"If you men ride out there, you'll be criminals," the sheriff continued. "I'll lock up the whole bunch of you."

"You jail them now!" Belizaire shouted at the sheriff. "Jail them now, do you hear me?"

The sheriff went on issuing his feeble, unenforceable order, and Belizaire continued to demand the vigilantes be arrested on the spot. Willoughby, whip in hand menacingly, took a few steps toward Belizaire with Meaux and Mouton close by but he neither said nor attempted to do anything to him.

Losing his temper over what he saw was a losing battle, Belizaire stormed over to one of the mounted vigilantes and beckoned to him. "You up there, off your horse now! Come on!" he shouted.

He grappled with the man, pulling on his leg, as the vigilante fought him off, slapping at him with his riding glove. On a command from the sheriff, Theodule and another deputy grabbed Belizaire's arms and pulled him away, still shouting and protesting.

As the two men held him fast, Belizaire watched in anger as Meaux and Mouton led the vigilantes off. As they rode away, Willoughby gently slapped the butt of the whip against the palm of his hand, smirking confidently that the mission he'd ordered his men to undertake would be carried out.

James Willoughby (Stephen McHattie) listens to some words of advice from the sheriff (Loulan Pitre) outside the Perry estate. (Photo by Michael Caffery)

CHAPTER NINE

Framed

SITTING IMPATIENTLY ON a bench in the sheriff's office, Belizaire was determined to force the sheriff into taking action to stop the vigilantes who had ridden after Leger. The sheriff was writing at his desk with a quill pen, uncomfortable with Belizaire's presence and his demands. He desperately sought rationalizations to justify his inaction.

"After all, it was your cousin Leger's choice to ride out of my parish," the sheriff argued.

"You don't need a posse," Belizaire insisted. "Lend me L'Ouragon. He's the only fast horse in the parish."

"L'Ouragon?" the sheriff asked incredulously. "L'Ouragon is parish property. Besides, he has a race Saturday."

"Well, do you want them to hang Hypolite?" Belizaire asked. His impatience rose with each refusal.

"I'll not start a war. Ask for something else," the sheriff said, going back to his writing.

Belizaire arose and stalked angrily out of the office. He could see that his efforts were futile. He headed across the street toward the stables and entered as if he had every right to be there. He untied L'Ouragon and began walking out with him, as the black stable boy made a feeble protest. Belizaire argued with him as he continued walking with the horse in tow.

"No, no. You got it all wrong," Belizaire told him. "I got express permission from the authorities to do what I'm doing."

Two other stable hands, older and larger than the boy, rushed out after Belizaire. One of the men grabbed him around the neck and dragged him away from the horse, while the second man led L'Ouragon back into the stable.

"Get your hands off me!" Belizaire protested as he struggled against the powerful arms clamped around his neck. Kicking and squirming desperately, Belizaire was overpowered as the man dragged him into the stable with him. Seconds later, a loud blow sent Belizaire stumbling backward into a pile of hay and stall sweepings. Seeing his cause was lost, Belizaire brushed himself off and sadly headed for home.

****

Out on the bayou road, Leger and his horse were beginning to show signs of weariness. Stopping by a shady grove of chinaberry trees, he dismounted and sat on the grass, fanning himself with his hat. The horse immediately lowered its head and began nibbling on some of the succulent grass at its feet.

A distant clopping sound interrupted their rest and he looked up through the trees to see Meaux and five other mounted vigilantes bearing down on his trail. Leaping quickly to his feet, Leger sprang over the saddle of his horse and spurred it away from the scene.

"That's him!" one of the vigilantes shouted, pointing toward the fleeing Leger. Shouts of "Hyaaahh!" filled the air as the armed posse began its chase of Leger through the woods and swamps, determined to bring him to the "justice" they had already "sentenced" him to.

****

The sheriff and Willoughby walked slowly across the vast lawn in front of the columned Perry mansion, passing under the low, thick limb of an ancient live oak. Nearby, ranch hands and slaves led horses around the property, going to and from their chores. The discussion between the lawman and Willoughby was tense as they went over the thorny legal issue of who would eventually inherit the plantation.

"Matthew and Alida were never married," Willoughby protested.

"Don't be too sure. Theodule may have forgotten about it," the sheriff answered. "I know I have a file on it somewhere."

"How large a bribe are you asking?" Willoughby inquired, realizing that he would have to play the sheriff's game.

"Matthew's children would inherit half the estate when old man Perry dies," the sheriff went on, baiting Willoughby with the sensitive subject.

"I know the law, sheriff," a testy Willoughby replied.

The sheriff stopped walking and began shaking his finger at Willoughby. "And to think I used to have to listen to people tell me you didn't want to learn our customs," he said.

After a long, tense pause, Willoughby asked "What exactly do you want from me?"

"I want to end the vigilantes," the sheriff answered quickly, getting to the purpose of his visit.

"That's not under my control," Willoughby said.

"When they come back from hanging Leger, I want them to find that I have caught Matthew's real murderer," the sheriff said.

Willoughby appeared nervous and uneasy. He tried to maintain a facade of calm as the sheriff continued. Did the sheriff intend to arrest him for killing Matthew?

"But all of my best witnesses are being chased out of town," the sheriff emphasized. "I need one of their own to convince them. I need you, Mr. Willoughby, as my witness."

Willoughby was thrown by this new turn of events. It was the last thing he had expected. Another long pause followed as the two men kept walking. Finally Willoughby turned, thrust his hands into his pockets, and asked who the sheriff planned to arrest. "You knew Matthew's enemies better than I did," the sheriff answered, tapping Willoughby lightly on the chest. "You choose."

He extended his hand toward Willoughby who stared at it for a few seconds. His own hands remaining in his pockets. Then he smirked, shook the sheriff's hand, and nervously scratched at a tic in his neck. The two of them turned and began walking back toward the mansion.

As the sheriff departed on his horse, Willoughby came around by the storehouse just in time to see Rebecca giving orders to a slave to hand Dolsin two pails full of milk. His face betrayed anger and Rebecca sensed it. She moved between him and Dolsin protectively.

"Hold on a moment! What's he doing here?" Willoughby demanded.

"We're not going to let them go hungry," Rebecca replied softly but firmly.

"Now if you think we're gonna provide . . ." Willoughby began, but Dolsin dashed off. The milk sloshed over the sides of the pails and spilled on the ground as he ran. Willoughby made a move to grab him by the shoulder. He missed, but Dolsin dropped one of the pails in his escape.

"Grab him! Stop him!" Willoughby shouted to the slave.

"No, James!" Rebecca shouted, taking hold of her husband's arm and trying to reason with him. He glared at her angrily. "We're not going to let them starve," she repeated.

Twenty feet away, the slave caught up with Dolsin and held him tightly around the waist, lifting him off the ground. The slave carried Dolsin in one arm and a milk pail in the other.

"Leave me alone!" Dolsin shouted, struggling and holding onto his hat. The slave ordered him to hold still and deposited him in front of Willoughby. Rebecca maternally looped her arm around Dolsin's shoulders, determined to protect him from her husband's unpredictable temper. Finally Willoughby began to calm down.

"I'm sorry, did I scare you?" Willoughby asked Dolsin softly, taking him gently by the hand and kneeling in front of him. He led the frightened boy toward the storehouse with his hand lightly on his wrist while Rebecca kept her arm on his shoulders.

"Come here. I want to talk to you. It's all right," he continued, taking off his hat and softening his voice.

"Do you know who I am, huh?" Willoughby asked the boy, who fearfully maintained his silence. "I'm your uncle, right? I didn't know who you were," he continued.

"Just give us a second here," Willoughby told Rebecca, and she reluctantly backed off a few steps. He leaned gently toward Dolsin, close enough to whisper to him without his wife overhearing their conversation.

"Your poppa's dead. Do you feel bad about that?" Willoughby prodded the boy, who began nodding his head up and down. "Does it make you feel just awful, your poppa getting killed like that? Do you know anybody who was giving your poppa any trouble? Anybody who might have killed him? Huh?"

Dolsin kept nodding his head.

"If you know, then whisper it in my ear," Willoughby implored.

Leaning toward Willoughby's ear, his head still nodding up and down, Dolsin whispered "Belizaire Breaux."

On hearing the name, Willoughby broke out into a triumphant smile and his eyebrows shot up. "How do you know that?" he asked.

"The night he killed poppa he came by our house," Dolsin whispered.

Willoughby stood up at once and motioned to a slave who was lounging idly alongside a buggy. "Go grab the sheriff! Bring him back here!" he shouted to the slave, slapping his hat back on his head.

"Should I get the boy more milk?" the other slave asked.

As he walked away, Willoughby deliberately kicked over the pail and the milk spilled onto the ground. Shaking the drops of milk off his shoe as Rebecca gasped in disbelief, Willoughby stalked back to the mansion.

"We can't let these bastards think they have any claim on this

place! Go grab the sheriff!'' he demanded and the slave by the
wagon headed off immediately.

Dolsin broke into a run. Unencumbered by the heavy milk
pails, he was out of the yard in seconds. Rebecca sadly watched
him go and turned her attention toward her husband who was
heading back to the house.

"No, James! Stop!'' she pleaded, holding up the front of her
long skirt and running after him. He stopped abruptly and faced
her.

"What's the matter?'' he asked impatiently.

"We are going to care for Matthew's children.''

"The hell we are!''

"You're not in charge here, James,'' she said.

"Well then, who is?'' he asked, his voice rising in anger. He
took three menacing steps toward her. "Matthew's dead, so if I
am not in charge yet, it won't be long. And when I am in charge, I
guarantee that those bastard children will not touch a head of our
cattle!''

"You're not in Mississippi anymore, James,'' Rebecca told
him. "The law in Louisiana says I inherit the herd. Not you. Not
us. Me! And when it is mine, I can do anything I like.''

"But that same Louisiana law says I am lord and master here.
Not you. Not us. And not those bastard children!'' Willoughby
sneered, raising his voice to a shout and shaking his finger at her.

Knowing she was defeated, Rebecca stood by helplessly and
watched him go into the house. On the second floor balcony, Old
Perry leaned on both the railing and his cane. The expression on
his face showed that he had heard the exchange between his
daughter and son-in-law. Saying nothing, but looking old and
tired, he turned slowly around and reentered his bedroom
through the balcony door.

****

In pursuit of Leger, Meaux led the other five vigilantes along a
trail that paralleled the bayou. Keeping their eyes on the other side

of the narrow waterway, they attempted to overtake the young man whose horse was galloping furiously just ahead of them.

"Which way, Meaux?" one of the vigilantes asked the leader. "He didn't pass by here."

Meaux looked around and made a quick decision. "Here. He went down in here through the swamp. *Allons!* Follow me. We didn't lose his trail. Follow me!"

He dashed his horse into the water, shouting "Let's go! Let's go!" to the other vigilantes. One by one, the men followed him, splashing across the bayou after Leger.

****

The sheriff, Willoughby, Theodule, another deputy, and three of the Perrys' slaves rode across a field on their way to Belizaire's house. Willoughby was alongside the sheriff, and the two of them conversed while the others rode behind in silence.

"I don't see what you're so worried about," the sheriff said to Willoughby. "We've convicted men with half this much evidence."

"I don't doubt it. I just wish I had some guarantee that you will keep your end of the bargain," Willoughby replied suspiciously.

"You have my word on it, don't you?" the sheriff said.

"Hah!" Willoughby retorted, indicating he didn't place too much faith in the sheriff's promises.

A short distance away, at his cabin, Belizaire was plowing corn rows with his mule. A frantic Alida, still in black mourning clothes, explained to him what was going to happen. She grabbed his hands and said, "Dolsin thinks you killed his poppa!"

"Alida, I got to explain to him that the stories people will be pumping into his ears . . ." Belizaire started to say.

"No, no! You don't understand, Belizaire!" Alida interrupted him. "He told James Willoughby!"

Belizaire clutched her hands. "Willoughby would never believe that I'm capable of . . ."

"No!" she cried, cutting him off again. "Willoughby is going to the sheriff! You must go now, Belizaire! You must leave! Please?''

Before he could answer, the sound of hoofbeats and snorting horses in his yard startled him. Reacting quickly, he knew that he must get Alida into hiding at once.

"Come here," he commanded softly as she began to panic. ''They'll find you here and they'll accuse you!''

Glancing over at his outhouse with the two crescent moons carved above the door, Belizaire shoved Alida toward it. ''You get in there!'' he ordered. ''Get in there and don't you come out!''

''Careful. Be careful,'' she cautioned as he held the door open for her and closed it behind her. Uncertain how to face his present dilemma, Belizaire's mind raced quickly and he finally decided to face it head on. He strode over to his front porch and stood there defiantly as the sheriff, Willoughby, and the others dismounted.

''That's him!'' Willoughby said to the sheriff.

Belizaire summoned up all his courage and remained standing on the porch as the group of men slowly began to close in on him. They approached him gingerly as if he were a dangerous criminal.

''I did not kill Matthew Perry!'' he bellowed, stopping the men dead in their tracks for a few seconds.

''How did he know we were coming?'' Willoughby whispered to the sheriff.

''And neither did Hypolite Leger!'' Belizaire continued.

''I know what you're thinking, Belizaire,'' the sheriff warned, expecting Belizaire to attempt escape. ''You don't stand a chance. You'll have to come with us.''

The sheriff nodded toward Theodule and his other deputy, directing them to make the arrest. Belizaire paced along the porch briefly, rubbing his beard, trying to decide what to do next. As the deputy and Theodule got within an arm's length of him, Belizaire suddenly bolted and raced up the steps that led from his porch to his attic.

''Get him!'' Theodule shouted to the other deputy and the two of them took off after Belizaire. Quickly scaling the ladder, they found the hatch shut tightly above them and they struggled in vain to get it open. The sheriff ordered his men and the three slaves to surround the house, and they scrambled around to carry out the order.

Theodule, gun drawn in readiness, entered Belizaire's cabin through the front door, accompanied by one of the slaves. Pushing aside the plants that hung down from the rafters, they looked around for another way to reach their quarry.

Outside the house, one of the slaves continued to try breaking through the hatch while the deputy, accompanied by another slave, spotted a ladder lying alongside the house. Raising the ladder off the ground, they leaned it against the exterior wall and the deputy climbed up toward a loft window that had the shutters closed.

He banged on the shutters and tried to pry them apart, shouting, "Open up!" Belizaire opened them, knocking the ladder and the deputy off balance. With a frightened yell, the deputy fell backward with the ladder as Belizaire tried unsuccessfully to grab hold of it. The deputy, still clinging desperately to the rungs, crashed through the palmetto-thatched roof of a nearby mule shed, landing heavily on the ground. Belizaire shook his head in apology and said, "That's too bad" as he closed the shutters again.

The other men rushed over to help the deputy and, in the commotion, Belizaire slipped out a side door. He cautiously eased his way toward the outhouse where Alida remained hidden. Sliding along the outside wall of the outhouse, Belizaire put his mouth close to a crack. "Are you all right in there, Alida?" he asked.

"Save yourself, Belizaire!" she whispered frantically.

By this time, Theodule and the slave who had been inside the house ran out and continued looking around. "Where'd he go?" Theodule asked. The two of them raced toward the outhouse, creeping along the opposite wall from Belizaire. Realizing he was close to being cornered, Belizaire made a quick dash toward the house and Theodule spotted him.

"There he goes! Go around the back!" Theodule ordered as he and the other men continued their chase. Ducking under a clothesline draped with Spanish moss hanging out to dry, Theodule and two others followed close on Belizaire's heels. Confused, frightened goats scattered in all directions.

Desperate to avoid capture, Belizaire leaped through a side window of his cabin, doing a perfect somersault, and quickly barred the window shut. Theodule and the others banged on the shutters, trying to get them open while Belizaire, temporarily safe inside, pondered his next move.

Theodule and the other men went over to consult the sheriff on what to do next. Belizaire cautiously slipped out the front door, eased his way along the porch, and peeped around the corner. He saw the men clustered around the sheriff and Willoughby, anxiously conferring. One of the slaves suddenly announced that he had to use the outhouse and walked toward it, untying his pants.

Fearing that Alida would be discovered, Belizaire reacted swiftly to draw their attention. "Yo!" he shouted, leaning around the corner of the house so they could see him.

"There he is! Get him!" Theodule shouted. The slave who was ready to use the outhouse forgot his need, and he took off in hot pursuit along with the others. Belizaire raced across the porch under his attic steps, and desperately began climbing his chimney. Stopping halfway up, he saw the sheriff and the others gathering on the ground below and he knew he was trapped.

One by one, Theodule, the other deputy, and the three slaves grouped themselves around the sheriff and Willoughby at the foot of the chimney. "Nobody shoot," the sheriff cautioned Theodule and the other deputy who had their guns drawn and trained on Belizaire. "We need him alive."

"Call the vigilantes off Hypolite!" Belizaire shouted.

"Too late for that, Belizaire," the sheriff announced.

"What is it you want of me?" Belizaire shouted even louder. "To say I killed Matthew Perry? Would that be enough to end this violence? All right then; I killed Matthew Perry! You hear me; *I killed Matthew Perry*! Now, you call the vigilantes off Hypolite!"

Alida, hearing his "confession" from her hiding place in the outhouse, lifted her head in amazement. Could it be true? Crying softly and covering her face, she remained hidden while Belizaire descended the chimney to be arrested, handcuffed, and escorted to jail.

After everyone had left, she quietly slipped out and made her way home. Sobbing and praying, her mind was now in total confusion. Was this man, whose life she had risked her own reputation to save, indeed her husband's murderer? She prayed it wasn't so.

Belizaire reads through his "confession" as the sheriff looks on. (Photo by Michael Caffery)

CHAPTER TEN

The "Confession"

INSIDE THE SHERIFF's office, Belizaire sat solemnly with a ball and chain loosely attached to the handcuffs on his wrists. He watched as the sheriff put the finishing touches on a written document with his long white quill pen. Behind him, Willoughby waited nervously on a bench against the wall. He was anxious to see the deal he had made with the sheriff carried out.

"Your confession is written, Belizaire," the sheriff announced, looking up and placing the quill back in its inkwell. "I'll read it to you."

"I'll read it myself," Belizaire retorted. The loose handcuffs around his wrists slid up to his elbows as he quickly snatched the paper out of the sheriff's hand.

The sheriff looked at him in disbelief. "I didn't know you could read," he said. Glancing behind him toward Theodule, he told his assistant to get the horses ready and Theodule quietly exited the side door.

Belizaire held the paper up toward the light so he could read better. He glanced slowly over it until he reached a passage that brought a look of shock to his face.

"Fathered . . .?" he asked, looking over at the sheriff in disbelief.

Willoughby stood up and walked over to Belizaire, leaning over him threateningly. "Yeah, that's right," he replied.

"This says that I fathered Alida's children," Belizaire said.

"Oh yes, you read very well," Willoughby answered sarcastically, "but you see, this is a legal document and that means . . ."

"No, Belizaire; it says that you were like a father to them," the sheriff broke in, emphasizing the word "like."

"No, it says that I fathered his children," Belizaire argued.

"The content of this sentence doesn't mean you're responsible," Willoughby said.

Belizaire, still outraged and protesting, began arguing the point. A shouting match erupted between he, Willoughby, and the sheriff. "You don't understand what you're reading!" the sheriff finally shouted above the other two.

"No, no! I'll tell you what this means. It means if I fathered his children, they could never inherit Matthew Perry's wealth!" Belizaire protested, glaring directly at Willoughby.

"No, it doesn't mean that at all," the sheriff said.

"That's the only confession I'll agree to," Willoughby declared, stalking around the room in disgust.

"You'll agree to? Now whose confession is it; his or mine?" Belizaire asked.

After a few more tense seconds the shouting died down. "Yours, Belizaire," the sheriff answered quietly.

"Then you take those words out," Belizaire commanded, shoving the document back across the sheriff's desk at him.

The sheriff just sat with his hands folded and didn't make a move to comply with Belizaire's demand. He glanced over at his pen but did not pick it up to strike out the offending passage. "What about Leger?" the sheriff asked Belizaire. "Sign and I'll send someone on L'Ouragon to save him."

Knowing his beloved cousin's life was at stake, Belizaire reluctantly acquiesced and grabbed the pen. The loose handcuffs clanked on his wrists as he signed the document. In order to save Leger, Belizaire not only admitted guilt for Matthew Perry's murder, but also acknowledged paternity of Alida's children. He shoved the paper back across the sheriff's desk with his signature on it.

Just as he did so, however, he glanced out the window and saw a stable boy in the street leading an old sway-backed horse with sickly looking hair that had been chewed up by insects. "Hey, you promised L'Ouragon," Belizaire said, standing up indignantly. "That's a plug!"

Sensing betrayal, Belizaire's mind raced and he knew he had to destroy the confession. Unhindered by the loose handcuffs, he snatched the paper before the sheriff or Willoughby could react, stuffed it into his mouth, and began to chew.

"Get it! Get it!" Willoughby shouted, grabbing Belizaire around the chest and pinning his arms. Belizaire continued to eat the incriminating document and refused to surrender it. He twisted and struggled with Willoughby while the sheriff tried to wrest the paper from his mouth. The sheriff finally managed to salvage most of it and Willoughby released Belizaire from his grip.

"So what if you and your cousin hang!" the sheriff shouted, poking his finger into Belizaire's ribs. "At least I'll save nineteen families from exile!"

Still munching on and swallowing the piece of the confession he'd managed to chew off, Belizaire looked at him disdainfully. His trust in the lawman, never very great to begin with, was even more badly shattered.

* * * * * * * * * *

Out in the swamp along the road leading south, Leger frantically spurred his horse through the shallow water, trying to stay ahead of the determined vigilantes pursuing him. "Hyaaahh, hey!" he shouted at the horse, snapping the reins against the side of the animal's neck. The fear he felt for his life was painfully etched across his youthful face, as he glanced back at the armed posse closing the gap on him.

Racing around cypresses and tupelo gum trees, Leger finally found the trail along the bank and steered his horse onto it. Only a

ehind, Meaux and the other vigilantes raced
hrough the swamp, hot in pursuit. Whipping
...ney emerged from the water and continued their
the trail.

* * * * * * * * * *

Inside a crude wooden cell, Belizaire was dressed in rags with his bare feet propped on the bed on which he sat. Even with the handcuffs still around his wrists, he still had enough mobility to softly play his accordian. The instrument whined its tune and Belizaire skillfully manipulated the bellows, humming along with the tune.

Thin lines of daylight outside seeped in through the single barred window some nine or ten feet off the floor and through the cracks between the planks. Diagonal supporting boards held the vertical planks in place, and on one of these supports, next to the steps that led down from the sheriff's office, Belizaire's hat hung from a peg.

The clicking sound of the door being opened drew Belizaire's attention, and he looked up to see the sheriff and Willoughby entering his cell. The sheriff descended to the bottom step and glanced impatiently at Belizaire who looked back at him as he laid his accordian aside.

"We're going to get Leger," the sheriff announced. "Theodule and I are rounding up a posse. What did you want, Belizaire?"

"You know, I've been doing a lot of thinking," Belizaire said, rubbing his beard and making it clear that his remarks were directed at Willoughby. "If I confess that I fathered those children as we say, I should leave something to provide for them."

Willoughby and the sheriff looked at each other, puzzled. Willoughby, who had been standing on the top step, descended and took off his hat as he approached Belizaire. "What exactly is it you want?" he asked.

"Oh, just a cow," Belizaire calmly replied.

"A cow?"

"A milk cow. A good producer."

"Alida will need milk for the children," the sheriff told Willoughby, nodding his head toward him.

"All right. I can let you have a cow," Willoughby said, nodding and reaching into his jacket pocket. He withdrew a small notebook, took out his pen, and started to write in it, but Belizaire was not finished.

"A mule, maybe," Belizaire continued.

Willoughby stopped writing and looked up, a puzzled expression crossing his face. "You mean you're not going to leave her your mule?" he asked.

"Oh, my mule is enough to keep me in corn, but her with the whole family to support like that . . ." Belizaire explained.

"Give him a new mule," the sheriff said, tapping Willoughby on the shoulder.

Willoughby pondered nervously for a few seconds. "All right. That's one cow and one mule," he said, writing in his notebook.

"Boy, I sure would love to give her a horse," Belizaire went on.

Willoughby looked up angrily from his writing. "No horse!" he snorted. "She's got two mules already. She doesn't need a horse," he said as he continued writing.

"I know. I'm just saying I would love to give her a horse," Belizaire persisted.

"I'm not giving her a horse!" Willoughby shouted. "Why, you're supposed to take care of her, not me. I'm doing you a favor. I'm not giving her a horse."

"You're gonna give her the horse," Belizaire demanded. "You give her the horse or, in my last words from the gallows, maybe I'll just tell the whole population here how you and me killed Matthew Perry together."

Willoughby was shocked but he pretended to be unruffled. "Nobody'd believe you," he sneered as he went back to his writing.

"Oh, they'd believe me," Belizaire replied ominously. "Because a man who's going to hang anyway can afford to tell the truth."

Willoughby looked even more shocked and nervous.

"I'm not going to deprive a man of his last words for the price of a horse," the sheriff told Willoughby, shaking his head and resting his hand on Willoughby's right shoulder.

"The horse is not the issue here! I will not be made a fool of! Not by him!" Willoughby shouted.

"I'm hanging the man. What more do you want?" the sheriff asked. He was beginning to lose his temper over Willoughby's stubbornness.

"And not some little Creole pony either," Belizaire went on, wiggling his bare toes and stretching his hands out to their full shackled width. "I want a big, strong American horse," he added, shaking his fists to emphasize his point.

"Oh no," Willoughby responded, walking away and shaking his head in disgust. He climbed the steps and placed his hat on, adding "If you let that man speak from the gallows, you can forget about having me as a witness."

The sheriff, once again caught in the dilemma of trying to appease both sides in a bitter dispute, attempted to reason with Belizaire. "I must get rid of the vigilantes, Belizaire," he said pleadingly, pointing his gray hat toward Willoughby. "I'm sorry, but I need him."

"Well, if I can't speak from the gallows, I've got other ways," Belizaire answered, ominously hinting at an alternative means of getting his message across to the people.

"What kind of spell are you gonna cast in a ball and chain?" Willoughby sneered. Flashing a triumphant smile, he left the cell.

"Did you get what you wanted, Belizaire?" the sheriff asked as he prepared to depart. "He's a very rich man. You could have gotten two or three pigs real easy."

Belizaire didn't answer. As the sheriff got to the top step, he turned once again toward Belizaire and whispered, "And that curse—make it a good one."

Belizaire let a worried smile show through his beard as the sheriff left and the door was latched shut. He really didn't have his next move figured out yet. Looking over at his accordian, he picked it up and began playing and humming again.

Hypolite makes a desperate flight for his life through the swamp with the vigilantes in hot pursuit. (Photo by Michael Caffery)

CHAPTER ELEVEN

Vigilante "Justice"
in the Swamp

RACING FOR HIS life, Leger tried to spur his horse along the swamp-side trail, but the animal was tiring and slowing down. The over-worked beast was nearly spent and could go no further. Leger looked fearfully behind him and heard the thundering hoofbeats of the vigilantes in pursuit. He quickly dismounted and attempted to continue his escape on foot.

Taking Parrain's revolver out of the saddle bag, Leger slapped the horse's rump, and with a start, the horse jumped forward a few steps. Holding the gun aloft, Leger ran desperately into the water, splashing and slipping on the mud as he tried to reach the dense underbrush on the other side.

The vigilantes, with Meaux in the lead, stopped short as they saw Leger's white horse grazing and resting just ahead of them. "Hey, there's his horse," Meaux shouted, and two other vigi-lantes repeated the message down the line.

"Now we got him! He's on foot!" Meaux shouted excitedly as he dismounted to scout the area.

Out in the swamp, Leger held his gun aloft to keep it dry. He splashed through the water, looking back in fear as he slipped on the mud and stumbled over submerged cypress roots. Meaux, who was listening attentively for any unusual sounds, heard the splashing and leaped back on his horse.

"Come on! Come on! This way!" Meaux shouted, pointing and leading the chase into the water. The others followed quickly, shouting to their horses and to each other. "Come on! He's right around here!" Meaux continued shouting.

"This is it!" shouted one of the vigilantes riding behind him, as the pounding hoofs furiously kicked up water and mud.

Reaching a cluster of small trees, the vigilantes quickly dismounted and tied up their horses, with Meaux supervising. "Come on. Let's go! He can't be far because we were right behind him!" Meaux continued to shout.

Lashing their horses securely to the trees, Meaux and the others took their guns out of their saddle bags and began their pursuit on foot. In addition to his gun, Mouton took a coil of rope out of his bag and followed close behind Meaux.

****

Back in his cell, Belizaire had gone back to playing his accordian until he was certain the sheriff, Theodule, and Willoughby had left. Then he decided it was time to make his move.

In the darkness of the cubicle, Belizaire lifted the ball shackled to his wrists and swung it heavily toward one of the planks. Grimacing as he released the heavy weight, he watched as the impact buckled the wood slightly.

Lifting the ball a second time, he carried it to the farthest wall of the cell. Rushing forward, again with a painful grunt, he heaved the ball and the plank gave a little more. He repeated the task a third time, and the board opened up at the bottom. Stopping for a few seconds to catch his breath, Belizaire gently lifted the board with his bare toes and pushed it out the rest of the way. He was free!

Racing like a madman across the street, the ball and chain weighing heavily on his wrists, Belizaire made a beeline for the stable and leaped aboard L'Ouragon. The horse's startled whinnies alerted the two burly stable men and the young slave boy, but this time Belizaire had a head start on them. Galloping the sleek black steed into the street with the stable hands running and shouting futilely at him to stop, Belizaire took off in the hope of saving Leger.

"Oh, it's you again," one of the stable hands muttered in disgust as he watched Belizaire racing away.

Across the open prairie, Belizaire desperately spurred L'Ouragon on. The ball and chain were a handicap to him and the handcuffs made it difficult for him to hang onto the reins. He was fatigued by the long, tense days he had recently been through, but Belizaire went on, fighting the forces pulling on his body. He was possessed by only one thought: to prevent the murder of his cousin by a group of desperate men acting outside the law.

****

Plunging through the swamp, Leger was up to his waist in brackish water, the green duckweed on the surface making a path for him as he plowed through it. Racing against death, gasping for air, he took off his hat and tossed it in the water, trying to stay ahead of his pursuers.

Finally, Leger saw he could go no farther. He took refuge behind a huge cypress knee to plead for mercy. Meaux and the other vigilantes caught up to him and were soon within shouting distance.

"Leger!" Meaux shouted, directing the other men into a flanking maneuver aimed at surrounding their quarry. "Give it up, Hypolite!" Meaux shouted again.

"I left!" Leger shouted back. "You told me to leave and I did!"

"You killed Matthew Perry and you're going to hang for it!" Mouton hollered, holding up the coiled rope for emphasis.

"I didn't kill him!" Leger said.

"You said you'd kill him the night he whipped you," another vigilante said.

"He hurt me, but I didn't kill nobody! I stole a cow, but I didn't kill nobody!" Leger answered.

Hiding behind the trunk of a thick cypress, Leger fired a wild shot in his panic. The report sent frightened crows cawing and scattering from nearby trees, and other birds sounded the alarm as well. The vigilantes instinctively ducked and hit the water, not knowing which way the shot was heading.

Abandoning his shelter, Leger broke into a run; then he turned and fired another wild shot. Slowed down to the point of exhaustion by the the thick swamp muck, his capture was a foregone conclusion as the vigilantes continued gaining on him.

"Give yourself up, Leger!" a young black-bearded vigilante shouted.

Leger ducked behind another large cypress, took careful aim, and fired again, but he didn't hit anyone. The vigilantes continued to close in on him, moving from tree to tree, as Leger fired still another wasted shot.

Finally, in desperation, he fired two more shots, neither of which had any effect. "I'll go to Texas!" he yelled. "I'll go farther than Texas! I'll go to Mexico!"

Meaux and Mouton moved in quickly on him. They heard the other vigilantes shouting to them to hold fire and take him alive, but they were too bent on vengeance to comply. Leger fired his last shot and looked on in horror as Meaux, a sinister grin between the two pistols he held aloft, got within twenty feet of him. Mouton moved up as close to Leger as Meaux was.

Leger stepped out of his hiding place, holding his pistol up, and pointing it toward Meaux. He clicked it and the barrel was empty. Meaux continued bearing down on him like a hunter approaching a wounded deer.

"Please don't. Please?" Leger pleaded hoarsely. "I'll go."

There were more shouts of "Hold your fire!" but Meaux paid no attention to them. Taking careful aim within point-blank range, he fired a shot from each pistol and they struck Leger on both sides of his chest. The impact spun him around and, as he fell face down in the water, Mouton fired a shot of his own, striking Leger's shoulder.

As the other four vigilantes caught up with them, they could only shake their heads sadly. Leger's lifeless body floated face down, his blood mingling with the green duckweed, creating an eerie hue on the surface of the water.

"This is not a firing squad; it's a damn turkey shoot," the dark bearded vigilante said.

Meaux stood watching the body for a few minutes to make certain that Leger was really dead. Then he gave an order, and Leger's corpse was dragged through the water back the way they had come. Draping Leger's body across his still-waiting horse, the vigilantes slowly made their way back toward town.

Though still hampered by his ball and chain, Belizaire nonetheless had L'Ouragon going at full speed toward the swamp. Following a parallel trail, he passed the sheriff, Willoughby, Theodule, and the five other men in the posse. They recognized him and shouted for him to stop. but Belizaire ignored their order and rode on.

A minute later, Belizaire caught up with the vigilantes as they returned slowly from their fatal assignment. They seemed as if they were in a funeral train. When they saw Belizaire racing toward them, they quickly drew their guns, but Belizaire swung his chain and the heavy ball knocked Meaux's gun out of his hand onto the ground.

Riding up to the horse that was carrying Leger's body, Belizaire jumped off L'Ouragon and began laying his hands all over the corpse, hoping to detect some sign of life. At the same time, the sheriff and his posse closed in on the group and ordered them to disarm.

"You've got no right here, sheriff!" Mouton protested.

"You men; throw those guns down!" the sheriff shouted. "Throw down those guns, I say! Throw 'em down now!"

"It's not your affair, sheriff," another vigilante said.

"Throw 'em down!" the sheriff ordered. "What have you been doing here?"

One by one, the vigilantes reluctantly threw their guns to the ground. The sheriff ordered Theodule to pick them up and put them in a pile. Seeing that Mouton still had his gun, the sheriff pointed and said, "Theodule, take that gun away from that man."

As Theodule approached Mouton with his hand outstretched, the vigilante looked as if he might shoot rather than give up his pistol. After a few tense seconds, however, he conceded and angrily thrust it at Theodule, who added it to the pile.

.Theodule and the other deputies walked around to the other vigilantes, taking guns from saddle bags and completing their sweep of the remaining weapons.

Belizaire untied Leger's blood-soaked corpse from his horse and dragged it over to a nearby tree, struggling with the dead weight and the additional burden of the ball and chain. Laying his hands on the young man's body, he wept as he administered some semblance of last rites. Sadly he said goodbye to his cousin. He dipped his finger in a nearby puddle and made the sign of the cross on Leger's body.

Still mounted at the head of the group, Meaux shouted, "Damn you, Willoughby!" Feeling betrayed, he glared with hatred at his employer who sat silently at the side of the sheriff.

"You men are murderers!" the sheriff railed at them.

"An execution is not murder," the vigilante captain answered defensively.

"Killing an innocent man is murder and one of you will have to hang for it!" the sheriff shouted back.

Gathering up his ball and chain, Belizaire slowly stood up and walked away from Leger's body toward the sheriff. The sheriff climbed down from his horse and walked toward him.

"Belizaire, which one of these men do you want to see hang with you?" the sheriff asked.

Without answering, Belizaire paraded up and down the row of vigilantes, piercing them with his icy gaze, and making them visibly nervous. He walked over to the pile of guns and sat down beside it, inspecting them meticulously.

Sniffing the barrels and opening the chambers to see which ones had been fired recently, Belizaire tossed the pistols and rifles with all their bullets in them over to one side. He found the two belonging to Meaux and the other belonging to Mouton, and saw that they were missing bullets. He rubbed his fingers inside the barrels and licked them, tasting the freshly detonated gunpowder.

''Those,'' he announced dramatically, tossing the fired weapons off to the other side.

The sheriff instructed Theodule to keep the fired guns separate from the others until he could determine whom they belonged to. Announcing that they were all under arrest, he ordered the vigilantes to move on, and the entire party made its way back to town. He and his men kept their guns trained on them to prevent anyone from escaping.

Escorted by a deeply grieving Belizaire, Leger's body brought up the rear of the tragic procession.

Alida tries to save Belizaire from hanging himself as Amadee Meaux (Jim Levert) looks on from the gallows. (Photo by Michael Caffery)

CHAPTER TWELVE

Drama on the Gallows

SIX WEEKS AFTER the Leger murder and the subsequent trials and convictions, a gallows was erected in the street outside the Vermilion Parish courthouse. Three nooses dangled ominously above the eight-foot-high wooden scaffolding where Belizaire and the two vigilantes were scheduled to be executed. A crowd had already begun to gather, waiting.

Inside, in his cell, Belizaire fingered his rosary, saying the appropriate prayer for each bead. The sound of the door opening interrupted his meditation. He looked up to see Theodule usher in Alida. Since Matthew's death, she dressed entirely in black. Her face was drawn, tormented with grief.

Theodule closed the door behind her. Belizaire and Alida stared silently at one another for a few seconds. Finally, with a nod toward her abdomen, he said, "You've got that pointed belly. Your boy grows well."

Maternally placing one hand, then the other, over her womb, she smiled and said softly, "His name will be Belizaire."

Belizaire smiled proudly. "Belizaire, eh? Well, he'll give you trouble," he chuckled.

"I wish you could be there to treat him," she whispered sadly, turning her face to the wall. The absurdity of Belizaire's upcoming walk to the gallows, this second death to add to her grief, welled up inside her.

"Why a confession, Belizaire?" she exploded suddenly, turning away from the wall and walking toward him. "I could have proven you innocent."

"To save Hypolite," Belizaire said.

"You didn't save Hypolite."

"No I didn't, did I?" Belizaire mused wistfully. "Hypolite, all alone out there. Stopped the men who took the law unto themselves. Well, all that a man's life is worth are his deeds. And yet they come from thirty miles around to see me hang for my prayers. But I have no deeds. I have no deeds."

She leaned on his shoulder. Touching his face lightly with her hand, she whispered, "The people will mourn their healer."

"Maybe not," he said softly. The light of an idea grew in his eyes. "Maybe not."

Outside in the street, the crowd around the gallows continued to grow. The barouche carrying Old Perry, Rebecca, and Willoughby pulled up and parked where they could have a good view of the hanging. Townspeople looked at them in their fine clothes and muttered resentment.

Alida, coming out of the courthouse, looked over at the barouche. When Willoughby caught her eye, she glared angrily at him. Easing her way off the porch, she hustled down the steps and quickly made her way off.

The priest entered Belizaire's cell in his full vestments, holding a Bible in one hand. As he and Belizaire embraced, the sad, troubled expression on the priest's face clearly relected his torment at all the violence in his parish.

"Father," Belizaire said as they stepped apart, "I've just sent someone for my last batch of the balm you need for this shoulder. It should keep you for quite some time. Let me see that."

"Thank you, Belizaire," the priest said softly.

He walked around to the back of the priest and began massaging his shoulders vigorously. The priest grimaced in discomfort as

Belizaire rubbed and rotated the joint where the right arm connected with the shoulder.

"I've also given some thought to your other problems," Belizaire continued.

"My problem? I'm here about your problem, Belizaire," the priest answered.

"No. I mean the one with the bishop," Belizaire went on, beginning to unveil his scheme. "A triple hanging is going to be terrible news, even in a place like New Orleans, eh? I'm sure he'll have heard about that."

"The diocese already wrote me about it," he replied.

"Father, wouldn't the bishop be proud if that young American landowner who was murdered—that Matthew Perry—let's just say that he was the very Protestant that you had converted to the church."

"A convert?" the priest asked.

"Married in the church. Yeah. And you baptised his children, remember?" Belizaire hinted.

The priest looked at him for a few seconds, then finally caught on to the implication.

****

The crowd continued to grow in the street as the execution drew nearer. Women walked among those gathered around the gallows, selling food and souvenirs out of their baskets. It was a great social event, despite its grim consequences for three men.

Theodule and several other deputies stood guard on the front porch of the courthouse, rifles poised, should any of the vigilantes try to free their co-conspirators. Amadee Meaux was the first to be led out of the sheriff's office, wrists bound securely with rope. The crowd reacted swiftly, booing and jeering the young man who had once been one of them until he aligned himself with the hated vigilantes.

William Mouton was the next one to emerge, also bound at the wrists. He was given the same treatment from the decidedly partial villagers.

The two vigilantes were led through the crowd where they were reviled and spat upon by those who felt oppressed by them. Making their way up the steps of the gallows, led by armed deputies, Meaux and Mouton were directed to their positions on either side of the platform. Nooses were loosely draped around their necks by a black-hooded executioner. The third noose, the one in the middle, was reserved for Belizaire.

As the sheriff escorted Belizaire out the door, spontaneous cheering broke out among his many friends in the village. Theodule left his sentry position to join the sheriff in escorting Belizaire through the crowd. Hands reached out to touch him and wish him well in the next world. He strained his own hands to reach them, but they were too tightly bound. Men and women crossed themselves and uttered soft prayers as he made his way to the gallows.

Belizaire walked between them, fearful, looking around for faces he might never see again. The sheriff and Theodule led him up the steps of the gallows, where he was placed between the two murderers. A noose was looped around his neck with sufficient slack for the time being. The executioner stepped back morbidly for the signal.

Rebecca and the elder Perry sat in their carriage and waited for justice to be done to the man who had confessed to killing their beloved Matthew. Willoughby, who had accompanied them, left and mounted the front porch of the courthouse to get a better view.

Pushing their way desperately through the crowd, Alida and Dolsin lugged Belizaire's heavy sack between them. It contained all the medicines, charms, herbs, and other paraphernelia of his craft that they had been able to gather from his cabin. When they got within fifty feet of the platform, they set the bag on the ground and waited for a signal from Belizaire to bring it forward.

A cheer went up through the crowd as the priest made his way onto the platform, and to its edge where he raised his arms in the air for quiet. The anxious buzzing quickly died down.

"Please, please," the priest began, "Of all this man's sins, his greatest was to defame the children of Matthew Perry."

Shouts of "No! No!" were heard scattered throughout the crowd. Alida glanced fearfully at Dolsin, unaware of what was coming next.

On the platform, the sheriff angrily stalked over to Belizaire, grabbing him by the shoulder and asking, "What's going on?"

"Hey, trust me," Belizaire whispered back.

The sheriff looked doubtful.

"Well then, trust the father," Belizaire added.

"I trust him even less," the sheriff replied.

"Please, please, one moment," the priest went on, trying to make himself heard over the hubbub of the crowd. "Matthew Perry and Alida Thibodaux, both of the Parish of Vermilion—Matthew and Alida were married by me when I first arrived here ten years ago."

The surprise announcement electrified the crowd gathered in the street below. On the barouche, Rebecca smiled triumphantly and looked back at her father, who showed faint signs of joy. Alida was stunned.

"That's a lie!" Willoughby shouted from the steps of the courthouse, angrily waving his hat in the air. "Don't believe a word that priest says! Get him off of there!"

Willoughby began pushing his way through the crowd toward the gallows to confront the man who was making the damaging announcement. The priest, however, ignored Willoughby's outburst and calmly went on.

"Due to special circumstances, one of them was newly-converted, and we did not publish the banns," the priest said. "We kept the wedding a secret."

Willoughby continued to push through the crowd in a blind rage. The sheriff, still on the scaffold, made a move toward the priest as if to stop him. Belizaire detained him by lightly grasping his arm.

"Hey, the widow Perry will need help getting into her new estate, sheriff," Belizaire whispered.

The sheriff stopped in his tracks and began giving some thought to the matter. "You know, Belizaire," he said, clasping him around the shoulders, "I've always wanted to get into the cattle business—on the side."

Belizaire winked at him as the priest continued with his announcement.

"The children are all his, all legitimate," the priest went on, referring to Matthew, but Willoughby's shouts interrupted him again.

"How does he know this, huh? It's a lie! Everything he says is a lie!" Willoughby protested, but the crowd drowned him out, wanting the priest to continue.

"They're all legitimate, and all baptized in our Holy Mother Church," the priest said, as Willoughby went on shouting, "It's a lie! Get him out of there!"

Taking their cue from Belizaire, Alida and Dolsin brought the sack forward to the edge of the platform. Willoughby went on raging, waving his hat in the air, and stalking through the crowd which was becoming increasingly hostile to him.

"He'll lie to you from the pulpit and he'll lie to you from the gallows! Lie!" Willoughby shouted. "How much did they pay you?"

"I hope this clears the whole matter up. Thank you," the priest concluded, making his way off the platform.

Willoughby continued ranting and raving as he paced back and forth through the crowd. Angry townspeople closed in around him threateningly. "This town doesn't need you!" one man spat out, hands on his hips as if daring Willoughby to pick a fight. Willoughby, declining the obvious challenge, turned away in disgust and went back to the courthouse porch.

Hoisting the heavy sack off the ground and struggling with it, Alida and Dolsin hefted the bag up to the platform. Belizaire, who was restrained by the noose around his neck and the ropes binding his wrists, was unable to assist them. Theodule and the executioner knelt by the edge and took the bag from them, laying it down at Belizaire's feet.

The crowd cheered as Theodule and the executioner unbound Belizaire's hands. Bedraggled but still triumphant, he smiled and waved, acknowledging the applause. Silence fell over the crowd as they prepared to listen to his last words.

"It brings me great sadness to be leaving this earth now," he began, eliciting groans and shouts of "No! No!" from his friends in the street below.

"As you know, I haven't even apprenticed my secrets of healing," he continued, only to be interrupted by more groans from those whom he would no longer be able to cure. Willoughby, suspecting more trickery and afraid of what incriminating words Belizaire might say from the gallows, came nervously down the courthouse steps again and made his way toward the platform. Belizaire continued.

"But before I go, I wanted to pass out these—just a little inventory of some of my medicaments and my remedies," Belizaire said, kneeling in front of the sack, with the sheriff looking closely over his shoulder.

"There's nothing here that's good without prayer, but those of you who could use it, it's yours," he announced. Reaching into the sack, the first item he withdrew was a square bottle filled with an aqua-colored liquid.

"This is an elixir for the breakbone fever," he said, sounding like a medicine show vendor hawking his wares. He was greeted at first by silence.

"And mixed with corn, this will cure the colic in a horse or a mule or an ox. Is there anybody here that can use it? Hey, anybody!"

"Belizaire, *moi*! Belizaire, *moi*!" a heavy-set man with a thick black beard announced, waving his straw hat in the air. Belizaire beckoned him to come forward and the man did. He handed the bottle to Theodule, who passed it down to the man.

Reaching into his sack again, Belizaire pulled out a small burlap bag sewn up around pulverized herbs. He waved it in the air and announced what it was.

"Here's a poultice for the snakebite, also good for afflictions of the gums," he added, spreading his upper lip apart to demonstrate its application. "And also for spider stings. Anybody?"

Several people responded, but Belizaire's eyes fell on Ozeme Guidry. "Ozeme!" he said.

"Yeah. For me?" Guidry asked as he came forward.

Belizaire tossed the poultice to him. "You remember me to your daddy. Maybe you have him cook up a nice big gumbo for everybody after I'm gone, eh?"

"Two gumbos," Guidry replied.

"*Lachez-les!*" someone in the crowd shouted, and applause quickly followed.

"Yeah! *Lachez-les! Lachez-les!*" Belizaire shouted back. It was a Cajun expression that meant "Cut loose! Have a good time!" but on this day it took on its literal meaning as well: "Set him free!"

Willoughby, though impatient, was somewhat more confident that Belizaire's last words would not incriminate him. He nudged a deputy aside and watched Belizaire's antics on the scaffold.

Belizaire went on giving away his wares, hawking them like a show vendor. Waving a bottle of liquid in the air, he gave his pitch.

"That's the most potent and popular elixir in the parish," he called out. "One drop in a glass of water to cure a cold, two for pneumonia. Who wants it? Who gets it?"

He spotted Sosthene running up toward him and whispered the old man's name softly. He tossed the bottle to him and Sosthene thanked him, saying goodbye in French.

The sheriff had ordered the vigilantes to sit together in the front row to watch the hanging, and they whispered nervously among themselves.

Rummaging through his sack, Belizaire pulled out a strange-looking item and announced, "Hey, that's a charm for the lonely. If you put it under the pillow of the one you love, it will bring a proposal of marriage."

He looked around the crowd until his eyes fell on the person he wanted to have it—a plump but attractive dark-haired woman dressed entirely in black. "Widow Comeaux, that's for you!" he called out.

The woman attempted to hide behind someone standing in front of her, but several people nudged her forward. Embarrassed and silent, she came running up, took the charm from Belizaire, and ran back without saying a word. The crowd cheered and whistled, embarrassing her even further.

As Belizaire went on hawking the remainder of his goods, Rebecca climbed down from her carriage and walked over to Dolsin. Kneeling in front of him and lightly taking his hand, she asked softly, "Dolsin, will you come sit in the buggy?"

He nodded and went with her as she gently led him by the hand. Reluctantly, casting a fearful glance at the elder Perry, Dolsin climbed onto the carriage and went to sit down in the seat opposite the old man. However, as he did, Perry pulled him gently down onto the seat next to him. Then he smiled, acknowledging his oldest grandchild for the first time.

Looking on in disbelief, Willoughby stared at the scene and went into a silent rage. He started to make a move toward the wagon to interfere, but Rebecca blocked his path with her arms folded. The determined look on her face told him that she was in command of the situation. Perry began asking Dolsin questions in an attempt to get to know his grandson.

Up on the platform, Belizaire pulled a bizarre-looking, twisted root out of his sack and held it up for everyone to see.

"This thing was given to me by a little old Santo Domingo slave woman," he began. "She called it the *gris-gris* of judgement."

The mention of the words "*gris-gris*" sent visible signs of fear through the crowd. Several "Oooohs" and gasps were heard as Belizaire went on with his explanation.

"But I warn you about it, because I've seen the effect of that root," he continued. "It must not be touched or played with by a little child. I've seen liars touch this and be stricken with the asthmatic fever. I've seen thieves touch it and they spit up their own blood."

More fearful gasps went through the crowd.

"I've been told that a man who has had the misfortune of taking another man's life, should he be in the presence of this root, he will be struck dead. I guess that goes for me too," he added.

He broke into a laugh and the crowd nervously laughed along. Still cackling, he shoved the root toward Mouton, who backed away in fear as far as the rope around his neck would allow.

"You want to touch that?" Belizaire taunted, shoving the root in Mouton's face a second time and playing on the condemned man's superstitions. Then he turned his attention to Meaux and did the same thing.

"How about you, Meaux, huh? How about you? Go ahead, touch it," Belizaire teased.

Meaux also backed away in fear, attempting to kick Belizaire. Belizaire, still cackling, shoved the root at him again, and this time Meaux's foot nearly connected. Belizaire then pushed the root toward the executioner.

"The executioner, he doesn't want to touch that, does he?" Belizaire asked the crowd. More cheering and laughing arose from them. Two sudden sneezes interrupted his presentation.

"Well, whoever wants that, let him take it," Belizaire said.

Fearful silence was the only response he got.

"Mr. Willoughby, I'm talking to you!" Belizaire shouted.

Willoughby came forward slowly, confused and uncertain what was in store for him. "*Gris-gris!*" Belizaire shouted, throwing the root and watching it land it at Willoughby's feet. The crowd gasped and Willoughby jumped back from the object.

"Now, why don't you touch that?" Belizaire challenged.

"I wouldn't dirty my hands," Willoughby retorted.

"Touch it!" several nearby voices ordered.

"You believe in it; you touch it," Willoughby shot back.

The man to whom Belizaire had given the first bottle of elixir, came up and shoved Willoughby toward the *gris-gris*, lying menacingly on the ground in front of him.

"Don't you touch me, boy!" Willoughby shouted, charging at the man and shoving him back. Another man pushed Willoughby back toward the root but Willoughby brushed him off. The angry crowd began to form a tighter circle around him.

"Touch it!" Belizaire again challenged Willoughby from the platform.

"I don't believe in black magic! That has nothing to do with me!" Willoughby shouted.

Belizaire began chanting, "Touch it! Touch it! Touch it!" and the crowd soon picked it up. Forming an even tighter circle around Willoughby, nudging him toward the root, the townspeople began to degenerate into an angry mob.

"You touch it unless you, and not I, took the life of Matthew Perry!" Belizaire exploded.

The crowd reached a fever pitch, shoving Willoughby toward the root, firmly believing this would get the truth out of him. Nearly everyone was shouting, "Touch it! Touch it! Touch it!" including the other vigilantes, the condemned Meaux, and even Rebecca. The elder Perry, glaring at the son-in-law he now knew was guilty of his son's murder, growled "Touch it!"

Stumbling along with an angry mob surrounding him, Willoughby lunged and broke through the circle, racing past the Perry barouche and knocking a man off his horse. Another man standing nearby made a move to stop him, but Willoughby was too quick. He was over the saddle in seconds. Whipping the horse with the reins in his desperation to escape, Willoughby made a mad dash through the crowd.

Belizaire, seeing what was happening, reacted quickly. With the noose still looped lightly around his neck, he moved up to the edge of the platform and waited. As Willoughby came dashing by, Belizaire timed his move perfectly and swung out on the hanging rope, knocking Willoughby off his horse with his feet.

In seconds, Willoughby was overpowered and subdued by a group of men in the crowd. Several deputies raced over and pointed their rifles at him. The sheriff, Theodule, and the executioner hustled off the platform toward the scene, and the sheriff placed Willoughby under arrest for the murder of Matthew Perry.

In swinging out, Belizaire had inadvertently tightened the noose around his neck. In the commotion he was left swinging painfully from the rope. Desperately he grasped the rope above the noose, trying to ease the pressure. His face began to turn purple as he gasped frantically for air. Alida came rushing over to help.

Swaying helplessly, his legs dangling, Belizaire struggled to get his fingers under the loop around his neck. With a superhuman effort, Alida lifted him up, holding him just long enough for him to get his fingers farther under the knot to loosen it. Finally he got it open wide enough for his neck to slip out and he crashed heavily to the ground, knocking Alida down with him.

Wheezing and panting, his face contorted with pain and his eyes wide open in fear of the death he had nearly suffered, Belizaire lay prone for a long, tense minute. Alida pushed hard on his chest and lightly slapped his face, crying, ''Breathe! Breathe! Breathe! Breathe!''

Finally, responding to her efforts, Belizaire was able to sit up. Alida's smile was one of relief; his was one of triumph.

CHAPTER THIRTEEN

Vindication and Reparation

LEAVING THE COURTHOUSE a few days later, a well-dressed Belizaire and the sheriff exchanged a few parting words on the steps. The sheriff pointed toward the edge of the pond across the street where Theodule and Jonathan, the Perry servant, were standing by a cow, a mule, and a horse. Alida and her three children were standing nearby, smiling at him.

"Now you're a man of means, Belizaire," the sheriff said proudly, relieved that the vigilantes' power had finally been broken. With two of the leaders dead and another condemned to share their fate, tranquility had once again returned to the bayou.

Belizaire nodded silently to him and shook his hand as he said goodbye. As he made his way across the street, Alida said a few words to Dolsin in French and firmly nudged him toward Belizaire.

"Go tell him what I told you to say," she ordered the hesitant boy. "Go on! Go on!"

Dolsin sheepishly came forward and lowered his head. "Mr. Belizaire, I'm sorry for all the trouble I got you into," he said in his soft voice, staring at the ground.

Remembering his brush with death and the harrowing events of the last few months, Belizaire shrugged off the apology. "No trouble," he replied nonchalantly.

Alida hugs Dolsin as Belizaire and the sheriff exit the Vermilion Parish courthouse. (Photo by Michael Caffery)

Thankful that his apology was accepted, Dolsin started back toward his mother, but Belizaire gently grasped him by the hand. Pulling him closer and draping his arm over the boy's shoulder paternally, Belizaire led him toward the waiting animals.

"Listen," he began, "I realize you were born in the fall of the year but, regardless of all that, happy birthday," he went on, pointing to the horse.

"For me?" the amazed boy cried.

"Yeah, that's for you," Belizaire answered, gently lifting him into the saddle.

Alida, holding Aspasie with one arm and Valsin with the other hand, looked on proudly as her oldest son took the reins of his first horse and gently led it around. Belizaire glanced back at her and nodded silently.

He made his way over to the cow, knelt beside the heavily sagging udder, and took hold of one of the teats. Squeezing it skillfully and squirting some of the milk into the palm of his hand, he tasted it and nodded approvingly. Standing up, he gently patted the cow on her rump and looked again at Alida, walking closer to her.

"I guess a year and a day you must mourn for Matthew." She nooded. "But the day after that will you marry me?" he asked softly.

She looked at him with soft, moist eyes and said nothing. Grasping Valsin's hand tighter and still clutching Aspasie, she walked ahead a few steps. He kept up a pace that put him a few steps in front of her.

"I've been thinking about that," he said, faltering over his words. "I mean, you'll need someone to provide for you, now that I'm a man of means."

He stopped and looked back at her, still waiting for his answer. "Maybe you'll be fixing to marry me?" he asked again.

Stopping under a low-hanging magnolia tree and letting go of Valsin's hand, Alida plucked off one of the large, fragrant, white blossoms and dreamily fondled it. Suddenly she was once again the beautiful young girl of ten years ago, entertaining proposals of marriage from nearly every eligible young man along the bayou.

She looked at Belizaire again but continued to withhold her answer, savoring the moment, allowing herself to feel the joy of still being attractive and desirable.

"Well, no harm in asking is there?" Belizaire persisted, letting out a nervous giggle.

Straightening himself up and putting on his most serious face, Belizaire looked directly at her and asked "Will you marry me?"

"We'll see, Belizaire," came the soft reply, as she glanced down instinctively at her bulging womb. "We'll see."

Staring at her nervously, twisting a small tree branch in his hand, Belizaire nodded. He knew that the answer he hoped for would come. Walking back over to the cow and the mule, he took the reins of both from Jonathan, nodded goodbye to Theodule, and began leading the animals along the street.

"Come along, my children," he said as he made his way off with his hard-won prizes. Crossing the footbridge that led out of town, Belizaire proudly walked away flanked by the two docile beasts of burden.

Dolsin trotted his horse closely behind him across the bridge, and Alida followed, carrying Aspasie and holding Valsin by the hand. Curious townspeople looked on in silence, smiling their approval. They were grateful that their healer was still alive and the beautiful Cajun girl, whom they thought they had lost might soon be one of their own again.

ABOUT THE AUTHOR

Born in 1955 in Cut Off, Louisiana, on the banks of Bayou Lafourche, Glen Pitre has Hollywood sitting up and taking notice of his work. A talented writer, film director, and producer, he brought all of the elements together for the making of the movie, "Belizaire the Cajun." The movie was a hit at the 1986 Cannes Film Festival, and scored rave reviews throughout its run in movie houses nationally and abroad.

After graduating from schools in Lafourche Parish, Pitre studied film, on a scholarship, at Harvard University. Graduating with honors, he returned to Cut Off and founded Cote Blanche Productions which he still presides over. Cote Blanche started out producing documentaries, educational films, radio spots, multimedia productions, and 16 mm Cajun French language docudramas.

In 1981, he had two Cajun movies touring southern Louisiana theaters, "La Fievre Jaune" ("Yellow Fever") and "Huit Piastres et Demie" ("$8.50 a Barrel"). They were shot in black and white and featured members of Pitre's family, based on stories handed down by the family. The two films made up a feature-length package that has also been shown in other French-speaking countries.

Also in 1981, he began development on a movie about a Cajun faith healer in the late 1850s who was caught in the middle of a feud between his fellow Cajuns and a vigilante group terrorizing them. Five years later, the film "Belizaire the Cajun" premiered.

Today, Pitre is working on scripts for several films, shuttling back and forth between Hollywood and Cut Off. *Belizaire the Cajun* is his first book.

ABOUT THE EDITOR

Dean Shapiro is a journalist, writer, and editor. He was born in New York City and earned his B.A. degree in history from Ramapo College of New Jersey in 1974.

Shapiro worked for several New York-area newspapers in the early 1970s and was a researcher for NBC News from 1975 to 1981. His credits include coverage assistance in the 1980 presidential campaign and the return of the American hostages from Iran the following year.

He has lived in the New Orleans area since 1981 and was the editor of several weekly newspapers, winning some of Louisiana's highest awards for journalistic excellence. He is presently associate editor at Pelican Publishing Company.